HANNAH & THE
SPINDLE WHORL

Hannah & the Spindle Whorl

Carol Anne Shaw

RONSDALE PRESS

HANNAH & THE SPINDLE WHORL
Copyright © 2010 Carol Anne Shaw
Third Printing June 2013

RONSDALE PRESS
3350 West 21st Avenue, Vancouver, B.C., Canada V6S 1G7
www.ronsdalepress.com

Typesetting: Julie Cochrane, in Minion 12 pt on 16
Cover Art & Design: Nancy de Brouwer, Massive Graphic
Paper: Ancient Forest Friendly "Silva" (FSC) — 100% post-consumer waste, totally chlorine-free and acid-free

Ronsdale Press wishes to thank the following for their support of its publishing program: the Canada Council for the Arts, the Government of Canada through the Canada Book Plan, the British Columbia Arts Council, and the Province of British Columbia through the British Columbia Book Publishing Tax Credit program.

Library and Archives Canada Cataloguing in Publication

Shaw, Carol Anne, 1960–
    Hannah & the spindle whorl / Carol Anne Shaw. — 1st ed.

ISBN 978-1-55380-103-0

    1. Vancouver Island (B.C.) — Juvenile fiction. 2. Salish Indians — Juvenile fiction. I. Title.

PS8637.H3836H36 2010   jC813'.6   C2010-901670-X

At Ronsdale Press we are committed to protecting the environment. To this end we are working with Canopy (formerly Markets Initiative) and printers to phase out our use of paper produced from ancient forests. This book is one step towards that goal.

Printed in Canada by Island Blue, Victoria, B.C.

for my mother,
who has been telling me
I could do this since
I was seven

ACKNOWLEDGEMENTS

A big thank you to everyone who listened to me prattle on for years about this book idea, and then left me alone while I wrote it. I am grateful to Ron Hatch at Ronsdale for his infinite expertise, patience and wisdom. A tip of the cap also to Erinna and Veronica for their copy editing. I couldn't have finished the writing without the unfailing support and friendship of Kristine Paton, eagle eye extraordinaire and fellow dreamer. Kris, I now fully comprehend the adage, "less is more." To my blueboarder buddies, you guys are great! Finally, my biggest thanks go to the men in my life: Richard, Trevor and Nick, who put up with the dust bunnies, mediocre dinners and my occasional crankiness. I love you guys. I couldn't have done it without you.

1862

THE FOG IS THICK and waist high. Moisture sits in the air, heavy and damp, and both the ocean and the sky are a deep slate gray. Gulls cry in the distance and, up on the point, a bald eagle screeches from the top of a tall cedar tree.

Yisella shivers, and draws her cape in close to shield against the cold. But she knows it's more than the damp that makes her shiver. Wind whips the surface of the water and sends a salty spray into the air, stinging her face. She narrows her eyes, and stares at the distant horizon, reassured now that nothing is out there. And yet, the dream will not fade.

Yisella pushes through the mist, keeping her basket close at her side. She has been lucky this morning — the basket is full of butter clams. She and her sister, Nutsa, will carefully dry the clams and prepare them for trading with the people who live across the water. These people also provide the rare and soft goat wool that Nutsa helps to spin for warm woollen blankets. Their mother, Skeepla, weaves the best blankets in their village. The best blankets in all of Quw'utsun'. Skeepla is known throughout the valley and all the way across the water. Yisella is proud of her village and its status among the island people.

As she makes her way over the rocks, the fog begins to clear. The first few rays of sunshine warm her hands and face as she nears her village of Tl'ulpalus. When she is closer to the village, she sees that several of the elders have gathered near the biggest longhouse. They are all admiring the freshly carved welcoming figure that's just been erected. Yisella joins them, carefully placing her basket at her feet.

The new welcoming figure is taller than any of the other carvings. The cedar tree, cut down and sacrificed for the figure, now stands straight and strong once again, its reddish hue rich against the colourless sky. His arms are outstretched to the sea in a gesture of friendliness, while his gaze scans the beach in front of him.

As Yisella makes her way over the driftwood, heading for the cedar-plank house where she lives, she turns for one more look. The arms of the welcoming figure cast long shadows upon the shore. He stands silent and still on this land warmed by the sun.

1
Cowichan Bay

MY NAME IS HANNAH. I live with my dad on a houseboat, the third one down on the left, dock five. I like the sea and I like falling asleep to the sound of waves slapping against the side of our houseboat. I sleep in a loft above my father's writing room. Yep, there's only room for my bed, my dresser, and a small table I use for drawing and homework — stuff like that — but that's okay. It's cosy and sunny, and when I lie on my stomach on my bed I have a perfect view of Cowichan Bay and all the neighbouring boats. I like the view best in the early morning, just as the sun is beginning to rise. The water is usually still, and the smells of coffee and hot muffins often drift over from the Toad in the Hole bakery, which sits on the shore. Skinny cats slink down the docks looking for boat decks to nap on after a long night of prowling behind the restaurants and bait shops. The first few cars headed for the larger cities, like Duncan or Nanaimo, begin to appear on the old road that snakes in front of the shops.

Our houseboat is made of scraps. Really. But it looks pretty cool. The cedar shakes were split from some logs taken off my dad's friend's property, and the windows were salvaged from a restaurant just before it was torn down. That's why my bedroom window has the words "Bird's Nest" written on it. That was the name of the restaurant. The rest of our houseboat is made from odd bits of lumber that Dad got from an old sawmill and Mr. Petersen's barn. We have a wood burning stove in the front room, and there's a funky winding staircase leading up to my sleeping loft. Dad built it out of twisted bits of driftwood. But the front door is definitely the best part. It's made of maple, and has a fern and periwinkle stained-glass window made by my Aunt Maddie.

My dad carved the posts and lintel out of clear yellow cedar. It took him almost a year to finish that doorway. It's full of carvings of all kinds of living things you might see in and around Cowichan Bay: sea stars, gulls, anemones, crabs, you name it. If you can find it on our beach, it's probably carved into our doorway. My favourite carving is the one on the top left, a little otter floating on his back in a bed of kelp. Sometimes in the mornings, when I'm watching out my Bird's Nest window, I've seen an otter just like the one on our door. He often floats on his back, too, between dock six and seven, and he's always curious about Ben North's fishing boat.

I could stay watching for a long time, wrapped up in my quilt, but then Dad usually bangs on the stair railing with a wooden spoon and yells, "Come on, Hannah, you'll miss your bus!" He says this almost every school morning and, of course, I always remind him that I never do.

The school bus stops just outside the Toad in the Hole bakery, so if I'm organized and ahead of time, I run down the dock and up the stairs and push through the screen door of the Toad where Nell is baking the last of the day's bread. I love Nell. She's pretty old, at least fifty. She has this crinkly face and wild grey hair. And she makes the best bagels I've ever had. If I'm really lucky, she'll push a hot cinnamon bagel straight into my hand before the bus comes.

The bus ride takes about twenty minutes and I usually sit at the back because I'm one of the first on. No one talks to me that much. I know that lots of kids think I'm kind of weird — probably because my hair is red and corkscrew crazy. And I live on a homemade houseboat with a father who writes in his sweatpants all day. Or maybe it's because my favourite shoes are boys' Wal-Mart black-and-white basketball high-tops, and everybody knows it isn't cool to wear those when you're a twelve-year-old girl. But I don't care. Not that much anyway. My running shoes are my favourite things, along with the lime-green knitted slippers Mom made me just before the accident. They're pretty ratty now and have tons of holes in them, but I wear them all the time because they remind me of her. I did have a best friend, Gwyneth, a while back. She was great. She made these amazing electronic gizmos and was a total science geek, and she never once made fun of my shoes! But she moved to Ontario six months ago so right now I'm kind of without a best friend. Michael and Wesley live two docks over on a big fancy houseboat, but they're more into fighting with sticks and playing zombie video games than exploring the woods with me.

I have this feeling when I get up this morning that it's going to be a different kind of day. Not an ordinary, go-to-school, come-home, eat-supper, do-homework, go-to-bed kind of day. Nope, I feel like something is going to happen. Don't ask me why. I just get these feelings sometimes. Dad says I'm "clairvoyant" like Aunt Maddie. I'm not entirely sure what that means, but I think it has something to do with being a vegetarian and wearing sandals in the winter.

But this is different. Like when I look out my window, everything looks really clear and blue, and sharp. What's even more strange is that I don't feel like lying in bed until the last minute, or writing one single word in my journal. And that's not normal for me. I get up right away, get dressed, and leap down the stairs to the kitchen where my dad is hanging over the counter, staring intently into the coffeepot.

"What are you looking at?" I ask him.

"The elixir of life," he tells me, scratching his head.

"Huh?"

My dad is always saying bizarre stuff like that and quoting famous dead people.

"The elixir," he goes on, "the tonic, the stuff of life, the ambrosia of the modern world, the— "

"Oh." I cut him off. "Coffee. Got it. Are there any waffles?"

"Waffles? Oh really? Her ladyship desires waffles, does she? On a school day, no less. Whole grain with fruit? Freshly squeezed juice to accompany your meal, madam?"

I get the message and reach for the Cheerios and milk. I decide that I'll visit Nell on the way to the bus and see if she's feeling particularly generous with the tomato-basil bagels. I'm just about through my cereal when Chuck, our orange tabby, jumps onto the table and starts in on what's left in my bowl. I don't really mind. Neither does Dad. I know some people who would totally freak out to have an animal on the kitchen table eating out of a bowl. Sometimes, when we have company, Dad goes into his "proper parent mode" and says things like, "Shooo! Chuck! What the devil are you doing, you crazy animal?" But more often than not, he'll give me a wink when no one's looking. Actually, for a parent, he's pretty cool. He does a lot of "wrong" stuff. Like sometimes, he lets me stay up late on a school night and read his work, and eat chocolate chips straight out of the bag. And once we had a food fight with spaghetti, and the tomato sauce ended up on the ceiling. He doesn't care about stuff like mud on your shoes or grass stains on your clothes.

Yep, things are a bit different at our place — Chuck is crazy too. For a cat, anyway. He'll eat anything. Cereal. Cold tea. Carrot sticks. Even cold mashed potatoes. And then he'll go to sleep in the laundry basket, on his back with his legs in the air. This morning I only have to fling him off the table once before he gets it and retreats to the laundry room.

2

Max

🎋

"I EXPECTED YOU TO stay horizontal for a while longer this morning," Dad says, finally sitting down with a mug warming his hands.

"I just felt like I needed to get up."

"I see. Women's intuition?" he asks. But he's got his head in a pile of papers already and I can tell he's having what he calls "a brainstorm moment." Which means that in a few minutes he'll only be able to say things like, "Uh — mmm — that's nice," without much enthusiasm. It doesn't really bother me. He is a creative genius, so it's allowed.

"Nope. I just get the feeling there's an adventure waiting for me today," I tell him, noticing that Chuck has already grown bored of the laundry basket and found his way back to the table. I carefully place a soggy Cheerio on the end of his nose. It sticks.

"Uh — mmm — that's nice," Dad says vaguely.

As I walk down the dock toward the shore, I can really smell the bread from the Toad in the Hole bakery. Raisins, too, which usually means cinnamon-raisin scones! I walk a little faster. When I stick my head in through the door, Nell has both her hands buried in a big green bowl.

"Hey, kiddo!" she calls out. She has flour in her hair, but it's hard to tell because her hair is pretty much the colour of flour anyway.

"I smelled cinnamon." I smile.

"Well, anyone up this early needs something to keep her strength up," she tells me, and hands me two big warm scones from a cookie sheet beside the biggest oven. "Here, one for each hand."

"Wow! Thanks!" I stuff half of one straight into my mouth; not exactly proper, but I just can't help myself. The raisins are warm and sweet, and I think to myself how much better the scones are than a lame bowl of cold cereal.

"Where are you off to so early, Han?" Nell takes a big jar of walnuts off a shelf by the sink.

"School, I guess. I just had a feeling I should get up early today. You ever get a feeling like that?" Then I feel really dumb because Nell is up half the night, baking all the delicious treats for the next day.

But she just chuckles and looks out the window for a moment. "Nope. Although I sometimes think I should lie in bed for about thirty-four hours straight and do nothing but read books and drink really good French coffee."

What is the big deal with adults and coffee anyway? Personally, I think it's gross. I'll never drink it. Not in a million years.

Nell and I chat for a long time, until eventually I hear the school bus braking just outside of Joe's Bait Shop. That means I have just five minutes of freedom left. I lean against the Toad's doorway until I see Wes and Michael coming along their dock, bashing each other over the head with their backpacks and yelling rude things at the seagulls.

Sabrina Webber is sitting at the front of the bus, just as she always does, scowling as usual. Sabrina never has a nice word to say about anyone, so I'm secretly thrilled when, after I sit down, she realizes that I've been watching her pick her nose for the last two minutes. She looks horrified. My intuition was right. It is going to be a good day!

Mrs. Elford is my grade six teacher. She's probably the best teacher I've ever had, except for maybe Mr. Butler, who I had back in grade four. He used to tell us stories of how he river-rafted down the Amazon with his brother and his German shepherd named "Ox." He could also juggle devil sticks and speak four different languages.

This morning in math, Mrs. Elford stops us just as we're about to start our page on fractions and goes to the door.

Mr. Wallace, our principal, is standing outside the door with a kid. After a few moments, Mrs. Elford brings the boy inside and says, "Class, we have a new student joining us today, all the way from 100 Mile House. This is Max Miller. I know you'll all make him feel welcome."

The boy has dark straight hair and is looking like he'd rather be anywhere but standing at the front of this class-room. I feel sort of bad for him because it must suck to have to start a new school in June when the year is practically over. He's wearing a green sweatshirt printed with a log cabin logo that says Flying U Ranch. His jeans are baggy and one of his shoelaces is untied. I can see Sabrina looking down her nose at him. Her shoelaces would never come untied in a million years.

"So, Max, do you have any brothers or sisters here at Elliot Elementary?" Mrs. Elford asks him.

"Yeah. I have a sister in grade three. Her name's Chloe," Max says quietly, and I notice he's kind of red in the face. Sabrina snickers into her hands and then looks innocently out the window when Mrs. Elford gives her a look. I see Max raise his eyebrow at Sabrina and then she goes red in the face too.

I think I'm going to like Max.

3

A Kindred Spirit

MAX SITS IN THE ROW beside me and I smile over at him. He looks grateful. When I'm halfway through the questions on page sixty-eight of my math workbook, I glance over again and notice the doodles on the edge of his notebook. There are beautiful drawings of a fish, a bear, a moose and a hummingbird. Each one is totally detailed and shaded, so it's only natural that a person would stare. But then I notice that Max is looking at me, and all of a sudden I feel like I'm spying or something.

"You're a really good artist," I tell him.

"Thanks," he says.

"How'd you learn to draw like that?"

"I dunno. I like animals, I guess. I watch them a lot."

"Have you ever seen a bear up close for real?" I ask.

"Hannah. Could you and Max save your conversations for recess, please?" Mrs. Elford smiles. Max and I roll our eyes and turn back to our math workbooks. When the bell finally goes for recess, Max sits with me near the monkey bars and tells me about the time, when he lived in the Chilcotin, that a bear came right onto his back porch and ate a forty-pound bag of dog food. I tell him about our homemade houseboat, and he doesn't think it sounds crazy at all. He thinks it sounds seriously cool.

I find out that Max and his family live at the other end of Cowichan Bay, in a house ten steps from the beach. His parents said that even though school was almost out for the summer, he had to start at Elliot anyway. They thought it would be easier to start grade seven in September if he knew some of the kids there first. When I ask him how come he wasn't on the bus, he tells me how his dad gave him a ride on his motorcycle. Cool. We hang out all day and by three o'clock I feel like I've known Max since the beginning of the school year.

"Want to come over tomorrow?" he asks.

"Sure."

Later on, just before dinner, I sit out on the deck with Chuck and open my journal — the one Aunt Maddie gave me for

Christmas. I've written in it every single day except a few days in February when I had the stomach flu. I love it. It has cream-coloured pages, a blue cover, and a pattern of shiny golden sun-faces all across the front of it.

Thursday, June 11, 2010
Dear Diary:

There's a new kid in our class. His name is Max. He seems kind of different, like he doesn't really care what kind of clothes he has on, and he's also really into animals and art. He actually seems pretty cool. Of course, I can tell already that Sabrina Webber doesn't like him, but she doesn't really like anybody . . . except Carl Norton. But I happen to know that Carl thinks she's a total idiot. I bet the only reason she likes him is because he's got a swimming pool at his house and a gigantic flat-screen TV in his own room. I sure don't see what's so great about him. He drools and always has gross sleep goobers stuck in his eyes. Plus he's got the personality of linoleum, as Aunt Maddie would say.

For supper, Dad brings out a tray of corned beef sandwiches made with Nell's whole grain bread. Hot spicy mustard and sliced dill pickles are already on the table.

"Well, Hannah Banana? What extraordinary thing happened to you today?" He's wearing bright green shorts and a T-shirt that says "When it rains, we pour" — advertising a coffee shop (of course, what else?) in Vancouver.

"A new kid started in our class today. His name's Max," I tell him, picking a sunflower seed out of my bread.

"Oh? So what's Max like?"

"He's kind of a slob, and his pants are too big."

"Ah. I see. A kindred spirit."

"DAD!"

"Truth hurts, eh?"

"Well, if I'm a slob, then I guess it's genetic, right? Oh yeah, Max's dad has a motorcycle. Can I go over to their place after school tomorrow? They live at the other end of the bay."

"Sure. I guess so. Just be home for supper, though. Aunt Maddie is coming over to cook."

Great! Aunt Maddie is my most favourite relative. She's my dad's sister and she's what a lot of people would call "eccentric." That means she isn't afraid to sing old Beatles songs really loud in the grocery store, and she wears pink and orange at the same time, even though my grandmother thinks it's a sin. Aunt Maddie likes to cook for us a lot; she thinks Dad doesn't feed me properly and stuff.

Later, when I crawl into bed, I pull my comforter up around my chin and listen for a while to the waves slapping against the houseboat. Then I take my journal out from under my pillow and continue where I left off this morning.

Later . . . but still Thursday, June 11, 2010

I almost forgot. I guess I was right when I woke up this morning. I knew something different was going to happen and it did. The whole Max thing. Oh . . . and Aunt Maddie's coming over tomorrow to cook again. That means there's sure to be tons of garlic involved! I'm glad she comes around a lot. I think it helps Dad because the last time she was over I heard him talking about Mom after I'd gone up to bed. He still misses her a lot even though he tries to hide it from me. But I think he's getting better because he's writing again. I mean, I miss her too, but I think it's kinda better for me not to talk about it all the time. Mostly, I just keep busy and try not to think about her so much. It's easier just to not go there.

P.S. I totally caught Sabrina Webber picking her nose on the school bus today. It was so sweet!

When I wake up the next day, Chuck is sitting on my head, anxiously waiting for his breakfast. He's like that. You have to feed him immediately or he'll dig his claws into your chin and start gnawing on your eyebrow. It's very irritating and impossible to ignore, so I get up and stumble down the stairs to the kitchen. My father has fallen asleep on the couch, again, surrounded by a pile of papers, and Chuck has discovered the bowl of melted mint chocolate ice cream on the floor. I go over, pick up the cat before he makes himself sick, and drop him onto my dad's chest. Chuck lands heavily and Dad wakes up.

"Whoa! Did I oversleep? I don't even remember going to bed. Oh, I guess I didn't. Geez, I hate falling asleep in my clothes."

"I think it suits you," I tell him, smiling. Dad's thinning hair is rumpled and his cheek is a roadmap of creases. My guess is that he pulled an all-nighter. He does that quite a lot when he gets his teeth into a good story.

I dump a smelly mess of canned chicken nuggets into Chuck's bowl, but he bumps my hand at the last minute and the whole mess lands on the kitchen floor. He doesn't care though; he just settles in to eat it straight off the linoleum.

"Are you going to this Max fella's house after school then?" Dad asks, reaching for the coffee beans in the freezer.

"Yep."

"No motorcycling though, okay?"

"Dad, I'm going to hang out with Max, not his dad." For a cool parent, sometimes he worries as much as a few fussy moms I know.

4

A Beach Day

❧

SCHOOL'S PRETTY BORING, but I don't mind too much because, well, it's Friday. The bell finally goes at five to three and I stuff my homework into my backpack and hurry to meet Max by the lockers. We climb on the bus and manage to score seats near the back, which is cool, because on the way home they usually get snapped up first. We don't say much during the ride; I stare at the forest which lines Cowichan Bay while Max draws a leopard gecko on the corner of his language arts binder. We finally get off just past Holly Ridge Bed and Breakfast. Max points out a house just past the corner store. It's a big white one with black trim and a deck that stretches off the back and out over the beach grass. We go inside, put our backpacks on the kitchen table, and Max pours us grape juice. He grabs a huge handful of oatmeal cookies; they're the really good kind — sort of undercooked and squishy in the middle. We sit out on the deck and eat about fifty cookies each before deciding to go and comb the beach for crabs and stuff, maybe make a fort out of some driftwood. That never gets old.

I love living near the beach. Even in the wintertime when it's raining, I still like to explore along the shore. The wind whips the trees back and forth and the ocean turns a slate-grey colour. But the best part is the fog. And the foghorn. It's kind of a sad sound, but, still, it makes me feel safe. I guess because I've heard that sound my whole life. When I was little, my parents and I used to sit out on the deck of our houseboat under the lean-to, and wrap ourselves up in blankets and watch the storms pass by. We'd usually drink hot chocolate, and Chuck would hide right under the blankets and not come out until it was all over. He's such a wuss. Sometimes there'd be an electrical storm, and we'd count the seconds between lightning cracks and booms of thunder to tell how far away the storm was. But most of the time in Cowichan Bay it's just whitecaps and wind and power outages.

Max and I make a really cool driftwood hut and there's enough wood left over to make a fenced area in front of it.

"I could totally live in one of these," he tells me, looking out to the ocean. There's a tugboat working really hard just a little ways off shore, pushing around a big barge out in the bay.

"What? You could? Even in the winter? Kind of cold, don't you think?" I decide that Max is probably a dreamer like my dad.

"Well, people used to live on the beaches like, a zillion years ago, in longhouses and lean-tos and stuff. With like, fire pits in the middle. I bet it was cool, eating smoked salmon and just chilling and stuff."

I think of the longhouse in the museum in Victoria, and remember the great smells of cedar and smoke. The chants that they play from some hidden speaker somewhere sound so real. Even though none of it is real, the forest at the museum is still my favourite part.

"Yeah, I bet there was a village right here on this bay," Max says. "They'd probably canoe over there to Kuper Island to trade stuff."

I look over the sea, trying to imagine what it would be like to see canoes there, paddling against the wind.

"And I bet there was more than one Bigfoot around here back then, too," he continues, his eyes kind of big and staring.

"You mean Sasquatch? You can't be serious," I scoff, sitting up straighter on the log.

"Oh yeah," Max nods. "Dead serious. Why? You're not a believer?"

"Is anyone?"

"Well, our neighbour in 100 Mile House said he saw one once when he was hunting moose."

"Get outta here."

"No. Seriously. He saw it take a package of hot dogs from his campsite, and he said its footprints were the size of trash can lids!" Max has told this story before. I can tell.

"Know what else?" He goes on before I can say anything. "I found an arrowhead once."

"Really? Do you still have it?"

"I had to give it to an archaeologist in Williams Lake even though I found it on Long Beach. It was a really big one, too." Max holds up his hands about six inches apart.

"It was kinda white, and sort of chalky."

All arrowheads I'd ever seen were shiny and black, made from that volcanic rock called obsiddy-something.

"The museum guy told me it was a trade item that actually came from the middle of BC somewhere. He said it was important that I found it on Vancouver Island, because it meant that the people here traded stuff with inland tribes in the Okanagan or something. The museum sure was stoked about it."

I wish I could have seen it. I love collecting things. The best thing I have is an orca's tooth. I found it on a beach on the mainland when I was seven.

"Why don't you do your report on that?" I ask him. We have to write our last report in social studies on something to do with British Columbia's history. Anything we want. "You could do some really wild scientific drawings with tons of detail and stuff too!"

"That could be pretty awesome. I'll think about it," Max tells me, checking his watch.

I notice that it is getting kind of late.

"Well, I guess I better get going," I say. "I think I'll follow the trail home from here. It only takes about twenty minutes. You know about the trail?"

"Nope," Max replies. "I haven't really had a chance to explore yet."

"It's great. It runs through the forest and comes out right across from the bakery at the other end of the bay. There are some really big trees in there."

We say goodbye, and I head off across the road and into the forest. The sunlight is filtering through the cedars, and the sword ferns on the ground are lush and thick. As I walk along, I decide that I really like Max. I like that he's sort of quiet and listens when you say something, even if sometimes it might be something sort of dumb.

A little Douglas squirrel darts across the path and runs up an alder tree, yelling at me the whole time.

"Chill out! I'm not trying to catch you," I tell him, but I hear him chattering long after I've gone.

I love walking in the woods. I like the way the forest floor feels under my feet when I run along the trail. Kinda spongy. And when it's dry, the moss smells warm and sort of sweet.

Like hot berries. Summer is pretty much here, and I can smell things growing. It's hard to describe it, but Aunt Maddie knows exactly what I mean because she'll say, "Yep. It sure smells like green out there!" Right away it makes you think of reading your favourite book while sitting on a warm rock at the beach and pushing sand between your toes.

I look up through the cedar boughs. Big puffy clouds are moving quickly across the tops of the trees. A wind is beginning to pick up and I remember that Aunt Maddie is cooking dinner. I start jogging briskly toward home.

5

The Spindle Whorl

MY STOMACH STARTS to rumble partway home, and I remember that I have a half-eaten granola bar in the pocket of my hoodie. I finish it quickly, and as I'm fumbling to get the wrapper into the pocket of my jeans, I'm thinking of dinner, and not really paying attention to where I'm putting my feet. I stumble over a twisted root and fly off the footpath, landing face down in the shrubs.

"Well, Hannah, that's what you get for thinking about spaghetti and garlic bread," I chuckle out loud to myself. Sprawled on the ground and feeling stupid, I squint my eyes and see that there's a big flat rock hidden beyond the bushes where I landed. I get up, brush off my knees and wriggle through the bushes, only to find a steep, ivy-covered embankment about fifteen feet high — definitely not visible from the trail. You can barely see the rock, it's so smothered by ivy; except, when I look a little more closely and walk to one end, I see a partially hidden opening close to the ground. It looks like the entrance to a cave. I can't believe it! The whole cave and the entire rock face are completely hidden from the trail. Unless you were to fall exactly where I did and shimmy under that same tangle of salal bushes, you'd totally miss it. I wish Max were here in case I get stuck or something, because I can't resist checking it out. I take a deep breath, get down on my hands and knees, and look up toward the sky as I suck in my belly. And there, up on the top of the rock face, staring back at me, is the biggest blackest raven I've ever seen! He's just standing there, checking me out with his beady black eyes.

"Uh . . . hi!" I say to him, because it almost looks like he's expecting me to start some kind of conversation. He actually answers me back. Well, sort of. He lets out a croaky squawk and then ruffles his wings, craning his head forward to watch me as I belly crawl through the opening. All I can feel is dirt and rocks and moss. I know right away that I'm going to have to come back with a flashlight, and Max. I'm not a fan of the dark, but I keep going anyway. There's a sliver of dim light coming from the opening I just squeezed through, and it smells like moss and mushrooms, or somebody's mouldy basement. I belly crawl another ten feet or so into the darkness, but then it gets so inky and still that I think better about going any further. This is freaking me out. I really hate the dark. I'm such a chicken that I won't even go on the deck of our houseboat after the sun disappears. For some dumb reason, I always think I'll either fall overboard or something, or someone might snatch me into the air. But this time, I will myself to suck it up because, despite my fear, this is wickedly cool!

And then my hand touches something behind a rock. Something smooth and sort of flat except there are ridges on it too. At first I think it's some kind of a shell, but then I realize that it's too big, not to mention too round! I spend a couple of minutes running my hand over the surface of the object. This is something I have to see clearly! I grab hold of it with both hands and begin to ease my body backwards and out through the cave opening. It's hard to crawl when you can't use your hands. A rock digs into the side of my hip and I wince, but I keep going. Once I'm all the way out, and my eyes adjust to the daylight, I pick up the strange round object and turn it over in my hands.

What is this? It's some sort of wooden disc. Again, I trace my fingers across the surface. It's pretty big — about the size of a dinner plate, and it has a perfect hole the size of a nickel right in the centre. But it's the designs on the surface of the disc that really amaze me. Fish. Two big fish, their arched bodies carved around the hole. It almost looks like the one fish is following the other one. The whole disc is heavy and smooth and I can tell that it's old. I study it closely. The wood grain is still noticeable, and the whole thing is a dark brown, kind of shiny in places, like the legs on our old antique coffee table at home. Something tells me this is really special. I feel stoked to have found it even though I don't know what it is. I think of all the times I've walked up and down this trail completely unaware that a cave lay hidden just ten feet off the path . . .

How long has it been here? How many other people have walked by without noticing it? I have my granola bar to thank for this. If I hadn't been thinking about food and supper, I would never have tripped and seen the opening myself. What is this thing I found? I wrap the object carefully in my gym T-shirt and put it in my backpack between my math workbook and my beat-up running shoes.

I can't wait to show it to Dad and Aunt Maddie. But I'm kind of creeped out too. Max and I had just been talking about artifacts and arrowheads and stuff, and then I go and find this! And strangely, the big raven is still hanging around. Only now he isn't looking down at me from his perch. Now he's on the ground looking up at me. He hops energetically from one foot to the other, and then struts closer. Right in front of me! When he hops onto my backpack, I step back quickly. What kind of a birdbrain is this?

"Hey!" I say, "Get off of that! What's with you anyway?"

Again, he squawks at me, ruffles his wings, and then flaps up to settle in the big cedar just off the trail.

I shake my head. Could this day get any more bizarre?

It starts to drizzle a bit as I near the end of the forest trail. I can see a few people on their boats, and there are even a couple of BBQs on the go — a sure sign that summer is here. All the windows of our houseboat are wide open, which can only mean that Aunt Maddie is already here and cooking up a storm.

I step out from the trees and onto the road. Nell has put the closed sign on the bakery door and gone home for a while. I can see all the day-old stuff bagged up, ready and waiting on the table by the door. I hope that Dad remembered to get carrot muffins. Aunt Maddie loves carrot muffins.

When I get home, Chuck is lying in the flower box under the kitchen window. There's nothing in it except a few clumps of hardened old dirt, but he doesn't seem to mind. He looks sleepy and bored and opens his mouth in a "hello" meow when he sees me, only nothing comes out. I can see Aunt Maddie by the stove. The counter is a complete mess, but we're used to kitchen chaos when she cooks supper. There are always vegetable peelings everywhere, and she uses every single pot and pan we own. We have to do dishes for about three days after she goes home, but it's totally worth it because she's such an awesome cook.

"Hey Aunt Maddie!" I call as I come through the door and chuck my backpack on the stairs.

"Hey Han," she calls back, brandishing a wooden spoon covered with tomato sauce. "Where ya been?"

"Wait till you see what I found!" And then I go cold all over, remembering how I had tossed my backpack on the stairs. What if the thing broke? I rush over to check and, luckily, it's still safe and snug between my books and my shoes. I slide it out slowly, like it's made of glass, and then flash it in front of Dad and Aunt Maddie.

"Holy cow! Where'd you get that?" Dad asks.

"I found it in this cave. In the bottom of this cliff, hidden just off the trail! I tripped and fell in the woods and I saw this rock face with a hole in the bottom covered by a bunch of salal and thick trees and ivy and stuff. So I crawled inside, and then I found this! Isn't it great! What do you think it is?"

"What do you mean, you tripped and fell?" Aunt Maddie starts picking twigs out of my hair and then notices the dirt on my clothes. "You crawled inside?"

Dad takes the thing carefully from my hands and examines it slowly, turning it over again and again. "Well, it's definitely a Native artifact . . . I don't think it's cedar though. It looks more like maple to me." Dad knows a lot about wood because of his carving hobby.

"Whoa . . . I bet it's carved from big leaf maple," Aunt Maddie says decisively. "This is way cool, Hannah. I think you've found a Cowichan spindle whorl. Coast Salish. And look here! Check out this pattern of salmon!"

When she was younger, Aunt Maddie studied anthropology in university and once even worked on an archeological dig in northern British Columbia. But now she works at home editing people's books. She does a lot of work for my father, because even though he's a very good writer, he's also a very bad speller.

"A Salish what?" I ask.

"Spindle whorl," she replies.

"A spindle whirl?"

"Not whirl; whorl . . . w-h-o-r-l. It was used for spinning wool and other fibre. It's what people used before spinning wheels came into use. I once saw a woman use one at a heritage fair. It was amazing. She really made the thing sing! She went into a sort of deep meditation. It was sure something to watch."

Now Aunt Maddie holds it, inspecting it from all angles, feeling the smooth lines of the carved images on its surface.

"Can I keep it, Dad?" I ask, then remember Max telling me about the arrowhead that he had to give to the archaeologist in Williams Lake.

"I doubt it, Hannah. It looks like something pretty important. We should let someone at the museum in Victoria know about this. It may be a big deal. They will want to examine this for sure and find out how old it is. Things like that."

"How do they do that?"

"Well, if it's really old, then they use radiocarbon dating. Dating the dirt, basically," Aunt Maddie explains.

"How old could it be?" I can feel myself getting more and more excited about the strange object.

"Well, hard to say. They say that people came across the

Bering land bridge during the last Ice Age and reached Vancouver Island close to ten thousand years ago," Aunt Maddie tells us.

"No way. Canada is only 142 years old!" I correct her. "We learned that in school last week. We learned that Confederation took place on, um . . . oh, just a sec! I can remember . . . we just had the test. Oh, yeah . . . July the first in 1867!"

"It's officially been a country for almost 143 years — and European settlers have been in eastern Canada for close to 400 years, but there's been human beings living here for much, much longer than that."

"Do you think it could really be ten thousand years old?" I ask her. I actually have butterflies in my stomach, and I'm already imagining the headlines in the *Cowichan Bay Gazette*:

LOCAL GIRL UNCOVERS ARCHAEOLOGICAL
GEM IN COASTAL FOREST!

"Ten thousand years old? Hmmmmmm. That's doubtful. Wood couldn't withstand that test of time. But it could be a couple hundred years old," Dad answers, resting his head on the back of our ratty green couch. "If it's been in a cave all this time, it would be somewhat protected from the elements. I think we should find out for sure, don't you?"

"Will they carbon copy it? I mean, radio — what's it called again?" I ask, looking at Aunt Maddie.

"Radiocarbon dating. Not if it's only a couple of hundred years old," she explains.

Then she starts going on about something called comparative analysis and other ways to tell the age of stuff that isn't super old, and I glaze over a bit because it doesn't really make any sense to me, and to tell the truth, it sounds kinda boring.

"Dad," I say, "when can we find out about this thing?"

"Well, I have to drive in to Victoria to see my publisher tomorrow. If you like, we can call ahead and try to get in touch with the museum. I'm sure someone there will want to have a look at this."

"Can Max come with us?" I ask. I KNOW that Max would be really excited to be a part of this whole thing.

"No problem for me. Give him a call, but I want to make an early start. If I can get in to see Ian before noon," Dad kids, "I have a good chance of being done before dinnertime." Ian Barker is the senior editor at Kingfisher Press. He's very gruff and tells my dad all the time how disorganized he is, how difficult it is to work with a writer like him, and how he should cut him loose — even though my dad has published four books with him. They're always arguing it seems, but they're good friends anyhow.

The smell of garlic wakes me from my daydream. I was right; Aunt Maddie has made her famous spaghetti and garlic bread. It's very spicy and she and Dad have dark beer with it, but I have to have milk. We eat on the couches with plates on our laps, and listen to Aunt Maddie tell us about her latest plans to go hiking in Nepal with two of her friends and a real Sherpa named Tashi. Apparently she met him when she was editing a book on the Himalayas. She's already running five times a week, and lifting weights to get fit before she leaves in September. Her biceps are pretty ripped, and after dinner she challenges my dad to an arm wrestle, and Dad loses almost right away. I feel kind of embarrassed for him, but Aunt Maddie just says, "Oh forget about it, David. It's probably just your writer's cramp acting up again!" which is actually a pretty cool thing for her to say.

Dad makes a face at her, but soon after, they both get serious and start talking about more boring stuff like income tax and accountant's fees, so I decide to call Max about tomorrow, and then just go to bed.

Friday, June 12, 2010
Dear Diary:

Well, diary? Today I found something that's even cooler than the orca tooth. Aunt Maddie thinks it's a Native spindle whorl! This morning I didn't know what that was, but now I do. It's a thing that was used a long time ago to spin wool. And this one might be Coast Salish, from around here! Aunt Maddie says there were even Coast Salish villages right here in Cowichan Bay. So, I wonder who it belonged to? Did they spin wool with it to knit slippers for their kids just like Mom used to do for me? Did they lie in their beds at night

and look up at the same stars that I'm looking at tonight?
Did they live in one of those cool longhouses that Max told
me about? Did they like to chill in the woods just like me? I
guess I'll find out tomorrow when we go into Victoria, that is,
if Dad can get us in to see someone at the museum.

Well, that's all for now. Pretty cool.

I shut the diary, turn off my light, and just start to doze off
when Chuck leaps in through my bedroom window and
lands on my stomach.

"Ow," I yell. "Can't you just land on the floor like a normal cat?" He ignores me, curls up at my feet and falls asleep
immediately. His paws are wet and he smells a bit fishy. No
doubt he's been snooping around Ben North's boat. In the
half-light, I can see the spindle whorl across the room, the
moonlight highlighting the beautiful carved salmon on the
smooth shape, which casts an odd circular shadow across
the wood of my table. After a while, the stars disappear and
it begins to drizzle again. I fall asleep to the sound of raindrops splashing against the tin roof of our houseboat.

6

Victoria Bound

❖

Saturday, June 13, 2010
Dear Diary:

I never really pay much attention to my dreams. I have them
all the time and usually they're kind of lame. You know, stuff
like I'm sitting in my room eating chocolate cake, or I'm riding
my bike somewhere cool, or I'm in a cold sweat because I
have to write a math test that I'd forgotten I had to take.
Occasionally though, I'll have a really good one — one where
Sabrina Webber trips and falls face-first in the mud, or gets
every question wrong on her English test . . . but most of the
time I forget them ten minutes after I wake up.

Last night was different. I went to sleep thinking about
the spindle whorl and then I had the weirdest dream. I
was in the woods bordering the beach, but something felt
really different. It was so quiet, and the trees were bigger,
and the air kind of crisper. Even the light was different.
I remember that my feet didn't make any noise when I
walked through the brush. I had a skirt on too, which is
totally stupid, because I never wear them. I seemed scared,
like I was hiding from someone, or maybe running away?
And I kept looking out to the sea, as if I were looking for
something. A boat, maybe? It was the sketchiest feeling.

When I woke up, I kind of didn't know where I was, or even
who I was. And the thing is, I can remember every single
detail, right down to the eerie drumming that I could hear in
the distance and this really cool big black raven that was
following me around for the whole dream. I mean, that's
freaky enough as it is after that psycho raven at the cave.
I remember feeling kind of comforted in my dream by the
sound of the drums. And then I woke up. Go figure.

I close my journal and shove it under my bed this time, behind the box of dolls and stuffed animals that I just can't
seem to get rid of. It's Saturday! I remind myself. I love Saturday mornings. Usually, I take my cereal and go out on the
deck if it's nice and warm. That's when all the other houseboaters do the same thing, and it can get quite chatty. After
about an hour, the whole shoreline wakes up, and the fish

market and the Toad start booming with people. Later, the weekend strollers swarm the craft stores and restaurants. Now that summer is pretty much here, the weekends just seem to get busier and busier. I'm glad to see all the action after months of rain and dark grey skies. Sometimes it gets a little bleak and lonely on a houseboat during winters on the coast. That's when I read a lot.

Today I toast an English muffin and go outside with Chuck. Sadie, Ben North's African grey parrot, is sitting on my dad's deck chair, preening her feathers. I like Sadie a lot, even though she always looks kinda shifty to me.

"Hey Sadie," I greet her. "Better watch out . . . there's a cat on board."

But I laugh out loud, because everybody knows that Chuck is terrified of Sadie. Maybe it's because she's too big to tackle, or maybe it's because she can imitate the bark of a Rottweiler, Chuck never sticks around when Sadie visits. Today he takes one look at her beady eyes and darts back into the house to take cover once again in the laundry basket.

"Kitty on a stick . . . Kitty on a stick!" Sadie mocks. It took Ben two months to teach her to say that.

I give her a piece of my English muffin and kick off my sandals. It's really warm for the middle of June. I can hear my dad bumping around in the kitchen, grinding coffee beans and opening and closing the fridge. He takes the wooden spoon out of the drawer and raps on the stair railing.

"Come on, lazy bones! Up and at 'em!" He calls to me.

"Too late! I'm already up!" I call back.

He looks outside sheepishly, and then adds, "Well, if you're up . . . where's my coffee?"

"Caffeine is bad for you. I don't want any part of your bad habits," I say, crossing my arms over my chest.

"Oh. Morning humour. How I love it," Dad says, shuffling outside wearing a navy blue sweater with holes in the elbows and a pair of jeans with paint on the knees. "I'm going to call the museum in an hour or so. You talk to Max last night?"

"Yep. I told him we'd pick him up on the way out. He'll be ready. He said he wanted to come with us even if we can't go to the museum. Just to, you know, hang out."

"Great. Make yourself useful for an hour or so, and we'll make a plan in a little bit."

He settles into a chair beside me. Sadie steps from the back of the chair to his shoulder and immediately begins preening Dad's hair . . . or, what's left of it anyway.

"Crazy bird," Dad says, smiling. "Why don't you go visit Riley. He's got enough hair to keep you busy till you croak." Riley Waters lives on dock nine and has a grey ponytail that hangs halfway down his back. Wherever Riley goes, a bag of shelled sunflower seeds goes too. There are often little trails of seed husks going from his houseboat to the bait shop, to the coffee shop, and back again. Sadie has yet to venture as far as dock nine, but if she ever discovers that head of hair, and a constant supply of sunflower seeds, she'll be in parrot heaven.

A bit later, after Dad calls the museum and gets the thumbs up from someone called Mr. Sullivan, he puts on better jeans, grabs his manuscript and travel mug, and yells for me to hurry up! I've learned that when Dad wants to leave, he means immediately. Nothing is worse than making him wait when he's got a plan. Waiting makes him really cranky and then he drives like a lunatic, so I hurry. This guy is going to meet with us, even though it's a Saturday, so it's the least I can do.

Our Jeep is pretty old, but it's very comfy, even though the stuffing is coming out of the seats here and there, and it kinda smells like an old tent. We've had it ever since I can remember. When I was six, Mom and Dad and I drove it all the way down to Arizona to see the desert. Both Dad and I have a thing about lizards. We saw lots of different kinds of geckos when we were there.

When we pull up to Max's house, his mom is on the front steps with Max's little sister Chloe. It looks like she's brushing Chloe's hair and putting it into braids. I kind of feel twisted up when I see that, because I remember Mom doing that to me just before she died. Dad looks over at me and I can tell that he knows exactly what I'm thinking. He chuffs me under the chin and winks. I feel like I have a giant grapefruit stuck in my throat. But then Max comes tearing up the walkway and climbs into the Jeep before I let my memories get the better of me.

"Hi Mr. Anderson. Thanks for letting me come along," he says as he climbs into the back seat.

Dad glances back over his shoulder. "No problem. It's nice to meet you, Mr. Miller."

"Same here. Hannah? Can I see the whorl?" Max looks eagerly at the floor between us where I put my backpack.

"Sure . . . check it out," I say, taking it carefully out of the old green towel and placing it on his lap.

"Whoa . . . this is awesome! It's hardly wrecked at all, except for this one bit here." He examines a part of a fish fin — an area where the grooves are smooth and flat with wear.

"Who's going to look at it?" he asks.

"Dad talked to him this morning. A man named Graham Sullivan. He's the head of . . . what is it again, Dad?" I ask.

"Archaeological acquisitions at the Royal BC Museum in Victoria. He was so excited about the whorl; he agreed to see us today, even though it's Saturday!"

I'm impressed and, even better, so is Max.

The Royal British Columbia Museum is next to the Parliament buildings right downtown near the water. After a visit, I love to sit by the totem poles in the park near the museum's entrance and watch the horses trot by pulling their carriage-loads of tourists. I wait for the carillon bells to chime in the courtyard.

We park a block away, near Beacon Hill Park, and walk over. We're about twenty minutes early, so we decide to use our family pass and wander around inside for a bit. Of course, I want to go into the simulated coastal forest and so does everyone else. I stand in the middle of the exhibit and try to figure out just how they make the light the way it is, as if it's really early in the morning and there's still a fine mist in the air. You can hear birds waking up and a wood-pecker tapping away in the distance.

I cross over the floor and hang over the railing to peer at the stuffed cougar the way I always do. It's kind of sad seeing him just lying there, all stiff and stuffed. What awful thing did he do to wind up in a museum, filled with saw-dust? But he's pretty convincing, even though his eyes re-mind me of the prize marbles I keep in an old pickle jar at home in my room.

Behind me is the grizzly bear, his huge claws made to look as though he is ripping apart a rotted stump in search of grubs. Each claw must be about four inches long. I hope I never get the chance to meet claws like those up close for real! There's also an elk standing among the maple saplings. He's almost twice as high as I am.

I've seen elk before, not too far from Cowichan Bay, up behind Shawnigan Lake. They're usually tagged because they're Roosevelt Elk, protected on Vancouver Island; it's illegal to hunt them, but sometimes people do it anyway. Not far from the elk there's this little red Douglas squirrel, like the one that chattered at me so angrily on the trail be-fore I found the spindle whorl. It looks like he's running down the trunk of a big cedar, and his tail is sticking straight up like a sail.

7

Mr. Sullivan

❧

"COME ON, GUYS, time to go," my dad whispers from the red velvet rope in front of the white-tailed deer exhibit.

We follow him out to the escalators and ride down to the foyer. The offices for the museum staff are in an adjoining building. Mr. Sullivan's door is open, but Dad still knocks before sticking his head in. Mr. Sullivan is sitting by a huge stack of books; he has a big beard and wears small round glasses. He's dressed in a turquoise T-shirt with a picture of a big Komodo dragon climbing up one side of it, faded jeans, and some seriously worn hiking sandals on his feet. All around his office are posters and photographs of dig sites, ancient tools, fossils, and artifacts and stuff. On the window ledge sits a sculpture of a South American native pan flute player and there's also a bunch of woven baskets on another shelf across the room.

"Ah, the Anderson clan!" Mr. Sullivan says as he gets up to shake our hands. "Glad you could make it. It's great to meet you."

His hand is warm and big and on his finger he has a silver ring with a bear carved into it. He sees me staring at it.

"Like it?" he asks me.

I nod.

"Tlingit. From the southern Yukon, up north," he tells me.

"Tling . . . I could never pronounce that," I tell him, and he laughs as we all sit down. Mr. Sullivan looks really excited, and keeps smoothing out his jeans over his knees.

"Well, let's have a look at what you've got there," he says, drumming his fingers rapidly on his desk. I reach into my backpack, pull out the green towel and carefully unwrap the spindle whorl. When I place it into his hands, he holds it without saying anything. Mr. Sullivan looks more serious now, as if he's looking up a really difficult word in the dictionary. Pulling a magnifying glass out of his desk drawer, he holds it up to the whorl, right in front of his nose. It takes forever before he says anything, and I try not to squirm in my chair.

"Well, Miss Anderson, what you've found here is something that many archaeologists could search for over their whole careers."

"Were we right?" I ask. "Is it a spindle whorl?"

"It certainly is. And you were also correct about it being Coast Salish."

"How old do you think it might be?" Dad asks Mr. Sullivan.

"Well, I can't tell you that right off the bat, but I would say that it could be close to one hundred and fifty years old."

"That's so cool!" Max says. "When can you tell us for sure?"

"Not until we've done further analysis," he says.

"Radiocarbon dating?" I ask, secretly pleased that I have a chance to use the term, even though I don't really know what it means.

"No," Mr. Sullivan explains. "Not this time. We only use that method on things that are much older."

"Just what is radiocarbon dating, anyway?" I can't help asking. I want to know. It just seems amazing to be able to find out that something you stumble on might be thousands of years old.

Mr. Sullivan explains, "Well . . . here's a simplified version. Scientists have been using this method for about sixty years. Radiocarbon dating measures the amount of carbon-14 in a fossil or artifact. Carbon-14 occurs naturally in particles in the atmosphere. As plants and animals use the air, their tissues absorb some of the carbon-14. After they die, they no longer absorb the carbon-14 and their tissues begin to decay. So, measuring the amount of carbon-14 left in a fossil tells us its age. The results are fairly accurate."

Max and I look at each other. I notice that one of his eyebrows is raised. He does that a lot, I've discovered.

"So is it true that there have been people living on Vancouver Island for, like a gazillion years?" I ask Mr. Sullivan, who is leaning forward over his desk and staring intently at the carved images on the face of the whorl.

"Well, human occupation of the east coast of the island goes back several thousand years," he tells us. "Archaeologists have found evidence of shell middens, what you might call mounds, as well as stone tools which prove that there have been people here for a long time."

"And radiocarbon dating was used to find out the age of that stuff?" Max asks, his eyes glued on a big stuffed owl that's sitting on the end of a bookshelf. I notice that it has the same kind of out-of-focus marble eyes as the cougar in the museum.

"That's right," Mr. Sullivan says.

"So were the first people here on the island spinning and knitting wool hundreds of years ago? Where'd they get the sheep?" I ask.

"Not sheep. Dogs," says Mr. Sullivan.

"Dogs?" I think of Quincy, Nell's dog, who is wiry, smelly and oily, and is constantly scratching himself. I can't imagine knitting a sweater out of his hair. I mean . . . I like dogs, and I like Quincy, but . . . gross!

"Not regular dogs. Little woolly white dogs. The Salish kept them specifically for their coats and sheared them like sheep. They're not around anymore; they became extinct long ago."

"And they knit sweaters from that dog hair?" I ask, wrinkling up my nose.

"Mmmm . . . it was weaving back then. On looms. The knitting didn't start until settlers showed them how," Mr. Sullivan says.

"The Cowichan sweaters!" I exclaim. Aunt Maddie has one, a gift from when she was at university.

"Yes. The Coast Salish were — are — great weavers, so it's only natural that they would take to knitting as well."

Max looks at me and grins. I know what I'm doing for my BC history report.

8

An Afternoon Downtown

WE STAY FOR ANOTHER half an hour, and I leave the whorl with Mr. Sullivan at the museum. It's an important find, and I wouldn't feel right keeping it all to myself. Discovering it was exciting enough. And what's just as exciting is that Mr. Sullivan and some other museum people want me to take them to the cave on Tuesday so they can do their own exploring. I ask if Max and I can come and hang out with them, and Mr. Sullivan insists that we be a part of the whole adventure. I can't wait. What makes it even better is that Max and I get to miss a whole day of school when we go.

We leave the museum and Dad suggests that Max and I

grab a bite from Market Square and then hang out in Chinatown while he goes to meet with Ian.

"I'll only be fifteen minutes or so," he assures us. But I know that he'll be at least an hour. The only person who talks more than Dad is Ian, his editor. I remind him of this, so we agree to meet in one hour by the stone lions at the entrance to Chinatown, on Fisgard Street.

Max and I head to Market Square, following the smells that drift over from Howie's Bagels. His bagels aren't as good as Nell's but, because we're starving, we order three: one each and one to split between us. We sit out on the top stair in the courtyard and watch a couple of little kids chasing a bunch of pigeons around in circles. There's a tall woman playing a familiar song on a twelve-stringed guitar outside the bookstore. She has a puppy tied to the railing beside her, and his ears flop over when he cocks his head to one side. It's like he's really listening to every word of the Crosby, Stills, Nash & Young song she's singing: "Teach Your Children" — one of my dad's favourite songs.

"Do you think there's more stuff in that cave?" Max asks suddenly.

"Well, I don't think there's that much room in there. I wonder why the whorl was in there anyway. It seems like kind of a weird place for it to be, you know?"

"Maybe there's a skeleton in there as well," Max says eagerly.

"Oh gross, Miller."

"Why? That'd be way cool."

"I was crawling around in there, that's why! I can think of better things to find in the dark than some old skull."

"You just don't have any sense of adventure," he kids.

"You're definitely twisted," I kid back.

We finish our bagels and cross the road to Fisgard Street, the start of Victoria's Chinatown. We both want to go into the famous never-ending store — a narrow shop full of twists and turns and strange and interesting angles. But not before we check out the grocery store with the pigs hanging in the front window.

"Now that's gross!" Max says to me.

At least we agree on one thing.

We spend about half an hour in the never-ending store. I buy a hinged wooden snake . . . I never get tired of them, even though I'm twelve. Max buys a deep blue silk wallet, the one with the peacock embroidered on the front. It's for his mom, for her birthday.

There are so many cool things in this place — you can easily spend two hours looking around and still not see everything. But we only have twenty minutes left so it isn't long before we're walking back up Fisgard Street to the concrete lions where we're supposed to meet Dad. Of course, he isn't there yet, but I'm surprised we only have to wait ten minutes before we see him loping up the street. From this distance, I notice that his jeans are too short. Flood pants. He's also mostly looking up at the sky. My dad's like that. Most people look straight ahead, or at the ground when they walk, but Dad looks up all the time. He says you miss a lot if you always have your eyes fixed on every step. Well, he might see more stuff than the rest of us, but he also has more accidents. One time he walked straight into a telephone pole and had a black eye for two weeks.

"Hi, Dad!" I call to him. "How was Ian?"

Dad doesn't say anything, just grumbles under his breath, muttering something about integrity and not selling out. I'm not quite sure what happened at Ian's office, but I'm pretty sure Dad that thinks Ian is wrong and he's right.

"You guys finished in Chinatown? Spend all your allowance, kiddo?" he asks me.

"Wait till Christmas and see," I tease him.

Dad wants to stroll up Fort Street and snoop in some old bookstores along Antique Row. His favourite bookstore is the one that smells like old cigars and wilting geraniums. Max is cool with that, especially when I tell him the owner's name is Arthur McNish and he's about two hundred years old. He usually offers me one of the partially unwrapped caramels he carries in his pocket. I'm pretty sure they've been in his pocket for at least twenty years because they're kind of sticky and covered with lint. I always take one, but I never eat it.

He never remembers my name, either. He calls me "Hilary" or "Helen," or some other "H" name. I used to correct him every time, but he always forgets, so now I don't bother. I figure that's okay. Anyone who has lived for two hundred years should be allowed to forget stuff like somebody's name.

He sure knows his authors though. He's read almost every book ever written on the planet, and always has a copy of some strange unknown title that Dad is hankering after.

Dad tells me that Mr. McNish used to teach English at a fancy university, and that he's got millions of dollars and two castles in northern Scotland, but he chooses to live in a seedy apartment over a drycleaner. I think that's pretty cool. He's also worn the same black Oxford shoes for eleven years. I bet he keeps all his money hidden in old cookie tins or under his mattress. I know this because I heard him say once how he hated bankers. He called them crooks. Dad says Mr. McNish has been writing a book about the history of his family, Clan McNish, for most of his life. It must be a pretty big book. Or a pretty big family.

While he and Dad talk about Scottish clans, Max and I explore the back of the store. No one can see us there so first we draw stupid faces in the dust on the shelves next to the fishbowl. In the history section, I find a book about Coast Salish culture. There's a picture on the front cover of a woman weaving a basket. Her hair is long and black and she's wearing a cape that looks like it's woven from the same grass as the basket she's weaving. I open the cover and a small spider runs out across my hand and disappears between two leather-bound books about railways. The book isn't in very good shape but it only costs three dollars. I check in my wallet and decide that it might be a good buy for my school report. Maybe it will even have something about spindle whorls too.

I hand Mr. McNish my money, and he puts my book in a brown paper bag with a grease stain on the front of it.

"There you are, Holly," he says, handing me the bag and my change. I smile and Dad winks at me. Max isn't even listening. He's got his face stuck in a book about graveyards and haunted houses.

"Thanks, Mr. McNish," I say, scratching the fat cat sleeping by the cash register. The cat opens one eye and mews faintly. I'm pretty sure it must be nearly as old as Mr. McNish.

After Dad buys three books, we head out onto Fort Street and back in the direction of the Jeep. I have to yank on Dad's arm halfway down the street to keep him from walking into a garbage can. He's too busy looking up at the crows watching us from the roof of the hobby store. Typical.

On the way home, Dad and Max talk about engines and houseboats, and the best way to eat crab. When Max says to my dad that he loves crabbing, Dad tells him he can catch a lot of them right off the Cow Bay docks. I let them do all the talking. I'm too busy thinking about Tuesday, when we're meeting Mr. Sullivan at the cave site, and wondering how I'm going to get through tomorrow and Monday. It's going to be the longest two days of my life.

Monday, June 15, 2010
Dear Diary:

Okay, now this is kinda creepy. More weird dreams about the woods again. Three nights in a row — with the drumming and the staring out to the ocean and stuff, only this time it was like I was watching someone else. Not me, but this strange girl, about the same age as me. On Saturday night, I dreamed I was kind of hiding in the trees, and I see this girl scurrying along through the underbrush. She keeps stopping to look through the trees, out to the sea and . . . it's like she's worried. She has something in her hands, but I can't tell what it is. And this big black raven, the same one as before, is flying above her head, just ahead of her. Is she following it, or is it following her?

I call out to her, to see if she's okay, but she can't hear or see me. It's like I'm invisible. I sort of follow her as she heads for this clearing beyond the trees. I feel like I know these woods, but somehow they're different. Darker, quieter, more still. Then, just before she gets to the clearing, I wake up. And, it's the same as last time: I can remember every single detail, like the sound of the quiet — if that makes any sense. So who is this girl? I can still see her face, and her black hair — the way it hangs down her back.

Then last night, after spending the day with Dad, scraping old paint off the deck, I had another one. This one was sharper and clearer than any dream I've had before. It's almost as though this dream picked up where the other one left off. It goes like this: I follow the girl into the clearing. I recognize it immediately, the shape of the beach and the stretch of mudflats where the tide has gone out. It's

Cowichan Bay. But there's a village there. A Native village.
Right near the beach. There aren't any boats in the marina.
There's no marina. But I know that's where I am. I follow the
girl to one of the village houses. It's made of planks. There
are two poles outside the door, painted with dull red and
black paint.

The girl goes inside, and over to a woman who is lying under
some blankets at one end of the house. I can see that the
woman is ill. There are beads of sweat on her forehead and
she's talking very quietly to the girl, in some language I've
never heard before. The girl keeps twisting this beautiful
turquoise and silver shell which shimmers like a rainbow
on a cord around her neck.

A fire burns in the corner in a shallow pit on the dirt floor,
and I see another girl, maybe a year or two older than me.
She has a bowl of something beside her. Another older
woman sits to one side of the sick woman. Her eyes are
closed and it's like she's chanting to herself. She makes
these strange gestures with her hands, and she picks up a
cedar bough and sweeps at the air over and around the
sick woman. And even though they don't know I'm in the
room, watching, I don't move. I don't make a sound. I barely
breathe. But I feel so sad inside, because somehow I know
that the sick woman is the girl's mother. And I know that
she is dying.

9

Adrenaline

❧

I MANAGE TO GET through Monday, which is pretty boring, except for when Sabrina Webber gets into trouble for writing something mean on Gemma Taylor's locker, and has to go see the principal. When she comes back into the classroom, she isn't smiling, but Gemma sure is. Other than that, it's pretty uneventful.

During last period, Mrs. Elford gives up trying to teach us about conjunctions and pronouns. Instead, we watch a DVD about the endangered marmots of Vancouver Island. She tries hard all day to keep everyone in line, but most of us are just too excited. Summer holidays are almost here.

"Dad," I say, just before I climb up the stairs to the loft on Monday evening.

"Mmmm?" he half answers. He's got a pencil stuck over his ear and there's an open bag of sour cream and onion potato chips on the paperwork in front of him.

"Do you think we'll find anything else in that cave tomorrow?"

"I dunno, Han." He swivels around in his chair. "Maybe some gold bars and bullion?"

"Daaadd! It's a Native site, not a sunken pirate ship."

"Well, you and Max just be careful. What if the cave belongs to Bigfoot or some other old cranky thing?"

"Bigfoot?" I sneer. "You mean the Sasquatch? Come on, Dad. You and Max are both obsessed with Sasquatches!"

Dad just raises his eyebrow at me and keeps quiet.

"Uh, Dad? Hello? You know that Bigfoot isn't real, riigghht?" It would be just like my dad to be a huge believer. He lives in a fantasy world most of the time anyway.

"Don't be so sure, Han," he says, hiding the grin on his face. "There are a lot of people who say they've seen one."

"Sure," I say, adding, "just like all the people who say they've been abducted by aliens!"

That makes him smile. "Just when did you get to be so skeptical, Hannah Banana?"

"Whatever. I just hope we find some more cool stuff tomorrow, not a stinky old Sasquatch guy."

"Well, unless you get yourself off to bed, you're not going

to find out, are you?" he says in his father-knows-best kind of voice. I blow him a kiss and climb the stairs, trying not to trip over Chuck as he weaves in and out of my ankles, mewing for more wet food.

I curl up under my comforter and look up at the sky. It's clear and the moon is big — almost full. The stars blink over the top of the mountains and I can see a satellite moving steadily across the sky above Mount Prevost. I wonder what kind of pictures it's sending back to earth tonight. Maybe there are some of me and Chuck wrapped up in my quilt, or maybe a couple of Dad scratching his head, chewing his pencil and making notes that no one else can read in the margins of his typed pages. A moment later, I hear Chuck purring and the clacketty-clack of Dad's fingers on the keyboard. The last thing I remember before falling asleep is listening to the music coming from the Baxters' place two boats down.

Tuesday turns out to be bright and sunny. The birds are singing really loud this morning — a sound I look forward to all winter. Chuck is already up, sitting on the windowsill looking hopefully at the little wren perched on the stovepipe of Ben's boat.

Dad is nowhere to be seen, but while I'm getting my cereal, I hear his feet coming along the dock outside. He has a newspaper under his arm and his sweater is on backwards with the tag sticking up under his chin — my father the fashion statement.

"Today's the day!" I tell him excitedly.

"Right . . . right . . . the museum thing," he says, beginning to unfold the newspaper. "Make sure you take the camera, Han . . . you may find some other stuff, right?"

"Good idea." Once again, I imagine the newspaper headline: Local Girl Discovers Important Archaeological Site. Only now, I'll also get credit for the photography. Sweet!

I'm too excited to finish my cereal, so I give it to Chuck. I stuff some things into my backpack and hurry out.

"Knock 'em dead, kiddo," Dad calls after me.

Outside, the air is still and the docks are sort of slippery from the dew. I jog down the planks and up the ramp, two steps at a time. I don't even stop in at the bakery to say hi to Nell. Max and I meet on the trail almost as soon as I cut into the forest.

"Where have you been?" he demands, looking impatient.

"What . . . it isn't even nine-thirty!"

"Well, I've been up and down the trail for, like, hours already! Geez . . . I never thought you would sleep in on a day like today."

"Chill out, Miller!" I tell him. "The team has to drive up from Victoria. Anyway, they said ten o'clock. We still have a whole half an hour."

"Whatever," he shrugs. "So . . . anyway . . . show me the site. We can go in first, and look around and stuff. I brought my flashlight." He waves a slim black Maglite under my nose.

"No, we can't. I promised my dad I wouldn't go in the

cave again until he or some other adult knows how to find it. And remember, Mr. Sullivan said to wait for the crew just in case we wreck something important trying to get in."

"Oh yeah," Max shrugs. "Well, show me where it is, anyway. I couldn't find it."

We walk quickly down the trail and talk nonstop about the possible finds inside the small dark space. It takes me a minute or two to remember just where to stop, and I have to backtrack to find the huge clump of salal.

"Here it is," I tell Max. "Look, you have to get down on your hands and knees, and . . . " I begin to scramble through — but then I stop, suddenly.

"What are you doing?" Max stops short before he bumps into me.

I don't say anything. I just look straight ahead on the ground, and then I turn slightly and look up into the bushes above me. It's spooky. Something feels funny . . . not quite right.

"Earth to Hannah! Whassup?" Max asks, sounding impatient again.

"Shhhhh, just a sec," I stall. I stare up past the salal into the giant cedar that looms before me. The breeze has picked up a bit and it moves the huge limbs of the tree, back and forth. They make a soft whispering sound. I hold my breath. I think I hear someone. I think I hear a girl's voice . . . a girl's voice calling someone, but I can't be sure, and then the feeling goes away — probably because Max is pushing on the back of my foot.

"Anderson! What's with you? Get going!"

"Uh . . . er . . . did you hear something a second ago?" I ask him. "Did you hear a girl's voice?"

"What? Are you nuts?"

"Okay. Never mind. Here. You have to get through this small space right here, and kind of tunnel behind this yew tree, and . . . are you with me?"

"Yeah, yeah, I'm right behind you."

"Okay, then, check it out." We brush off our hands and knees and stand staring at the wall of ivy before us. I point to the dark opening at one end.

"Whoa! COOL!" Max cries, walking toward it, craning his head down low so he can check out the entrance.

"Don't start messing around in there, Max. You might wreck something," I warn him, before looking over my shoulder and up at the cedars again.

"Oh yeah? Like a creepy skeleton of some old spirit dude? You're not freaked out, are you Hannah?" he teases.

"No! But you are definitely obsessed with creepy things and dead stuff."

"Nah — you're just chicken. I can tell," he says. "I can see it in your eyes." He looks like he's enjoying himself.

"Besides," he continues, "what's so creepy about dead stuff? Everybody's curious. Why do you think cars slow down at accidents? 'Cause it's a total gore fest! Everyone wants to get a good look!"

It feels like someone has just taken a sledgehammer to my chest. I can't breathe . . . Max's words . . . The car . . . they said it was a write-off. I remember the exact moment when the police officer came; how he struggled to find the right words to tell Dad and me what happened; how I couldn't believe that Mom was never coming home again. For a second I can see her face right in front of me. I can smell her . . . the lemon-scented fragrance she wore every single day. I feel like I'm going to fall over. Instead, I yell at my friend.

"Max! You stupid jerk!"

And then I'm shimmying through the underbrush to get out to the trail. I can't get there fast enough. In a flash I'm up and running. I don't know why, but I keep going. I run as fast as I can and I don't stop until I get to the clearing at the end of the trail, near the bakery.

I hear Max running up behind me. "Hannah! What's your problem? I don't get you."

I can tell he's mad. He must think I've really lost it. I just stand there, breathing hard, staring out at the ocean, unable to look at him.

"What's wrong with you?" He steps in front of my face and breaks my gaze, forcing me to look him in the eyes.

What's wrong with me is that I suddenly hate Max. I don't care about the stupid spindle whorl. Or the archaeology team. I don't care about the cave or my school project. I don't care about anything.

I miss my mom.

I miss my mom, so much!

10

The Dig

✳

"HANNAH?" NOW MAX looks more worried than angry. "Hannah, how come you're crying? Will you please tell me what's wrong? I don't understand."

Of course, how could he? He doesn't know that much about me. He was just goofing off; guys are like that. And I understand how it must seem to him since he knows absolutely nothing about my mom. So I take a deep breath, and I tell him everything, about how she died in a car accident almost two years ago. When I'm done, he looks like he wants to sink right into the ground.

"I'm really sorry, Hannah. I . . . I didn't know," he says.

"I know. It's okay."

"I just thought your parents were, like, divorced or something."

"It's okay. I mean, I'm okay. It felt good to talk about it." I smile and the tension vanishes. "Besides, I figured I'd better tell you, before I sucker punched you for being such an idiot."

"Oh really? Like you could, Anderson!" He gives me a good-natured shove and I trip him and knock him to the ground. We're both laughing when we catch sight of a big green pickup truck pulling up outside the bakery. The driver gets out first and I recognize Mr. Sullivan, wearing a grey sweater. As he grabs a backpack from the box of the pickup, another person, a woman, gets out. She's wearing khaki cargo pants and a Green Day T-shirt, and she looks pretty young. The last person to leave the truck is a tall guy wearing a hat. He looks real serious and I think he's younger than Mr. Sullivan, but it's hard to tell 'cause of the hat. Max and I run across the road to meet them.

"Hi there!"

"Good morning, Hannah. Hey, Max," says Mr. Sullivan. I smile and secretly hope they can't tell that I've been crying. I'm not a pretty crier. In fact, I look like a Hawaiian blowfish after I've cried.

Mr. Sullivan introduces Max and me to the team: Jim Williams is a speleologist — he studies caves — and an expert in the field of First Nations culture; Kelly Parker is a graduate student at the university. I can tell Max thinks she's cute by the way he tries to stand taller. And he's kind of staring at her dark wavy hair, piled loosely on top of her head, and the freckles scattered across the bridge of her nose.

We're ready to hit the trail but first Kelly darts off to buy juice and butter tarts from Nell at the bakery. She says she didn't have time for breakfast but I know it's the smell of those baked raisins that got her. Max watches her jog across the road and then he looks up at Jim and blurts, "Hey, are you Coast Salish?"

"Good guess. What was your first clue?" Jim teases, pointing to the hat on his head. Max reads the word *Quw'utsun'*, part of the Cowichan Cultural Centre logo embroidered in plain view on the front. He looks over at me and I can see his face turning red. I just shake my head and look away. Duh.

Then Kelly comes back and Mr. Sullivan says to me, "All right, boss, lead the way."

"Sure," I say, trying to sound calm, but I can't wait to get started. "It isn't very far at all."

Everyone is so anxious to see the cave that no one stops to look at anything on the way, so we get there pretty fast. I show them where to shimmy under and through the underbrush, one at a time, 'cause it has to be the exact spot. Within minutes, we're all standing in front of the ivy-covered rock face.

"Wow," says Jim, shaking his head. "That's been growing here for a while. Wish they had nabbed the twit who brought that stuff over on the boat!"

"What stuff?" I ask.

"The ivy," says Mr. Sullivan.

"Oh, I like it. It's pretty." I tell him my grandma has ivy covering the whole front of her house in Vancouver. There was even a robin's nest buried in it last spring. A turquoise eggshell fell out of that nest, and I still have it sitting on my dresser at home.

"It may look nice, but it's an introduced species. They choke out all the native plants, and they are impossible to get rid of once they start."

Jim studies the ivy for a minute or two and then checks to see what else might be growing in and around it. Mr. Sullivan tell us that Jim is also an ethnobotanist, and explains that this means he studies the history and use of local plants, especially where they grew and what the people native to the area used them for in ancient times.

Jim starts pulling away the ivy in one corner of the rock face, just over by the cave entrance. "Whoa . . . will you look at this?" he says excitedly.

"WHAT!" Max and I screech at the same time.

Jim carefully removes more of the ivy to reveal a dull red line on the rock. "I'm not sure but I think we might be looking at the edge of a very big pictograph," he explains.

"That's rock art, for us laypersons," Kelly laughs and pulls out her camera.

"For real?" I ask, stepping closer.

"For real," Mr. Sullivan confirms with a half-smile. He puts down his pack and tells us all to set about the business of removing the rest of the ivy from the rock. "Hannah, you and Max can start over there, slowly, and with care, like this."

"But what about the cave?" Max pipes,

"All in good time. First things first." Mr. Sullivan and Jim both say it at the same time. By the expression on Jim's face, and Kelly's, too, I get the feeling that it's one of Mr. Sullivan's favourite sayings.

Max and I take off our own backpacks and get to work. We pick up an ivy runner each and begin pulling it away from the rock, very gently.

About eleven o'clock, we all stand back to look at our progress. I can't believe what I'm looking at! Before us is a crudely drawn human figure — a girl — and not far from it, another girl. The two figures have their arms open to each other, as if they are going to hug or something. They're painted in a dull red, which is faded in spots, especially near the bottom. There's this big circle between them and it has a tiny circle in the middle.

Mr. Sullivan thinks that the ivy covering them all these years is probably what protected the figures from the elements.

"Maybe the ivy's good for something after all, then," I say, rubbing some dirt off the end of my nose.

"You could be right, Hannah," he says.

I pull out my camera and, together with Kelly, I take a zillion photographs of the rock art. Mr. Sullivan and Jim start talking seriously about site protection and funding. They also need permission from the Cowichan Band for a full-scale excavation. If there's enough money, Mr. Sullivan wants to involve the university's summer field school, which means Kelly gets to stay on.

"This is a very rich site," Mr. Sullivan adds. "We know that Tl'ulpalus village was only a stone's throw from here, very close to where your houseboat now sits, Hannah. There must have been some significance to this cave for that village."

"Why?" I ask.

"Because of this pictograph," Jim explains. "The locations for rock art carvings and paintings were chosen very carefully by the Coast Salish. These places were usually places of mystery, where spiritual forces were believed to be especially strong."

"This discovery is sure to excite a lot of people," Mr. Sullivan adds.

I look at the crudely drawn picture on the rock, and study the strange circle between the two figures. Could that circle be a drawing of my spindle whorl?

11
Voices

꙰

WE STOP FOR LUNCH and everyone is chattering at once about what this means for the museum and how it adds another piece to the puzzle of Vancouver Island's rich history. Mr. Sullivan fiddles around with his iPhone, makes a bunch of calls, and then scribbles some stuff in a spiral notebook. His handwriting is even worse than my dad's.

"What'd they use for that paint?" Max asks Kelly, before biting off a corner of his tuna sandwich.

"Mmmm . . . things like charcoal, and crushed shells, and berries and stuff. And they'd usually mix in fish eggs or animal fat to make it last longer."

"How'd they figure that out?" I ask. Who'd ever think that fish eggs would make paint last longer?

"Well, I guess the first people here had thousands of years of trial and error," Kelly explains. "Probably used oolichan oil too," she adds, pulling her hair into a ponytail. Max is staring at her again.

"Ola-what?" I ask.

"Oolichan. A tiny oily fish. Big staple food for the Coast Salish."

"Well, I've lived near the sea my whole life and I've never heard of them."

"It's true. They were a handy fish to have around. There aren't many critters that will help you write a letter before you eat them," Jim says, smiling.

I have no idea what he's talking about. Maybe all the excitement of the day has gone to his head. I think that Jim senses my confusion because he goes on to explain. "Ooli-chan. Candlefish. That's another name for them. So oily you could run a wick right through them, light them up and use them like candles."

"No way. Really?" I wonder if Dad has ever heard of them. He knows a little about a lot of things.

"Really," he assures me.

We talk more about fish and spirits and shamans and stuff. Jim tells us a few Coast Salish legends that are pretty intense and kind of spooky. Especially the one about Quami-chan, a wild woman who lived on Salt Spring Island, who ran around with a basket that she'd made out of a snake. She ate people, and would sneak into different villages at night and steal the children. Jim said that one time she hid a hundred little kids in a cave until she was ready to eat them for dinner. Then she invited her sister to come and help her cook them, but in the end she got pushed into a big fire and burned up. It's a pretty freaky story.

I move a couple of feet farther away from the cave after Jim tells that one! But, scary or not, I'm glad that I now know a little bit more about the people who used to live on the island and the stories they would tell.

"What about Sasquatches?" Max asks, out of the blue. Figures.

"What about them?" Mr. Sullivan says, sticking his pencil into the pocket of his sweater.

"Do you think they're real?"

"What do you think, Max?" Mr. Sullivan tries to look serious.

"I'm not sure. There was this guy — Richard Carr — that I knew in 100 Mile House, and he said he saw one when he was hunting."

"No kidding," says Kelly.

"He said it didn't try to hurt him or anything."

It's now my turn to raise an eyebrow.

"He told me," Max went on, "that the Sasquatch actually saved him from a rockslide. Wouldn't let his horse pass by this dangerous ravine."

"You never told me that part," I say, wondering if he's making it up to impress Kelly.

"You never asked."

Jim reties his bootlace and puts his hat back on his head. "Well, that's not too weird. Some people say Bigfoot has a good heart. That is, if you're a good person."

"Richard Carr was a pretty nice guy. He used to repair all the ranchers' fences up there for nothing."

"There you go," Mr. Sullivan nods. "You get what you give."

"Yeah," Max agrees, "in this case, Mr. Carr got to keep his life."

I look at them all like they're cracked. Sasquatches. Right.

When lunch is over, Mr. Sullivan, Jim, and Kelly start comparing notes and measuring stuff and talking in scientific terms, so I pull out my journal from the side pocket of my backpack and lean back against a cedar tree. Max finds a clearing a little farther down the trail and lies flat on his back with his eyes closed.

Tuesday, June 16, 2010
Dear Diary:

Well this sure beats sitting in math class at school. How many kids get to be part of a real archaeological excavation just minutes away from where they live? And everyone is so nice to me and Max. I think Max totally has a crush on Kelly.

She's the university student who's here too. I can tell because he keeps smoothing his hair and I could swear he's trying to make his voice deeper.

Anyway, Jim Williams — he's the expert — just told us some stories about the Coast Salish. There's this one legend that's really cool. About a woman who would eat children and fly through the air. It kind of freaked me out but at the same time you want to know more. Archaeology seems pretty fun, but there's a lot of boring stuff you have to do, too, like math problems and reading maps and looking at tons of data that just look like a bunch of jumbled numbers. That's why I'm writing now. They're all busy doing that kind of stuff (major yawn). Oops, gotta go — it looks like they're finishing . . . more later.

When the team has finished their notes, we get down to the nitty-gritty: checking out the inside of the cave. But I soon learn that it isn't as simple as turning on the flashlight and going in. It's painstakingly slow: pictures are taken, measurements are made, and soil has to be brushed aside using paintbrushes. The tiniest bits of rocks and stuff are bagged and labelled. Worth the wait though. Just beyond the place where I found the whorl, the cave opens up a bit and you can stand instead of belly crawl. It is totally cool.

After two solid hours, there are definitely some things to take back to the museum: bone fragments and two tool artifacts. One artifact is part of an adze, a tool with a stone blade, and the other one looks like a needle made from a piece of antler. There are a few shell fragments as well. Mr. Sullivan says there's a midden near the shore not far from here, and the bits of shell are probably from that site.

I can't believe it when Kelly says, "Hey, it's 4:30 guys. We should head back now, Graham, don't you think? Lots of people to see about this." Then she turns to Max and me. "And you guys have been wonderful! How does it feel to be responsible for a very significant archaeological find?"

"Are we famous?" Max asks hopefully. I notice that he's blushing a bit. Actually, he's blushing a lot.

"Of course you are!" Jim says slapping Max on the shoulder. "We wouldn't have any reason to be here unless your friend here had contacted us."

Kelly takes the artifacts and packs them carefully in sealed baggies with even more labels attached. Then she puts everything in a wooden box and adds some figures to a weird kind of graph. We walk back toward the main road on the trail, all of us tired, very dirty, and definitely hungry. I keep thinking about ancient feet wandering similar forest trails through Cowichan Bay. Where were they going? Who was at the other end? And all the time I'm thinking this, I have this feeling I can't quite explain. The same kind of feeling I had when I was showing Max the cave earlier. Then I hear it. The wind has returned, and I stop on the trail. There it is. The girl's voice again. It sounds familiar, like the girl in my dreams.

"Did you hear that?" I ask the others, stopping dead in my tracks.

"Hear what?" Kelly asks, looking at me, and then following my eyes up to the tops of the cedars.

"I thought I heard a girl calling someone. I heard it before. Earlier."

Kelly hesitates. "Nope. I don't hear anything."

We listen for a second or two more, but all we hear is a woodpecker tapping off in the distance, and a dog barking down at the marina. But it's harder to ignore this time. I know what I heard.

"Maybe it was him?" Kelly says, laughing and rubbing some dirt off the end of her nose.

"Who?" I ask, confused.

"Him!" Kelly points to a big black raven sitting on a stump just off the trail. "He's been hanging out there for a while. I noticed him earlier."

No way! Not him again. I totally get the heebie-jeebies, although Kelly seems unfazed by his presence.

"Weird," I begin. "He was there a couple of days ago, in the cedar tree, and before — on the rock above the cave opening. Watching me."

"Hmmmm. The trickster," Jim says. "Messengers of magic. Maybe he knows something we don't."

I know that Jim is teasing, but I secretly wonder if maybe he's right.

After we say goodbye to Graham Sullivan, Jim, and Kelly, I tell Max that I feel as though that raven has been watching me.

"You're nuts, Anderson," he says to me. "You just got freaked out by all that talk of Bigfoot and crazy witch women and stuff."

Maybe he's right. Maybe my imagination is working overtime. The crazy dreams. And now this. There has been a lot of talk about mythical animals, shape-shifting and, of course, those intense legends. That would get anybody's adrenaline pumping.

Max and I say goodbye, and I head past the bakery. Nell has locked up. I know she's still in there, but I don't bother telling her all the news because I know she's counting money and doing "the books," as she calls it. She absolutely hates it when people bug her between five and six at night.

As I walk down our ramp, I can see Dad walking down dock five with a newspaper in his hand. I can't wait to tell him about the day, and the photographs, and Mr. Sullivan, Jim and Kelly. Not to mention the stone tools and the pictograph. He's going to flip.

We spend the evening going over every single detail of the day. He wants to know everything. He doesn't go near his laptop the entire night and he even ignores his cell phone. That doesn't happen very often.

"You writing all this stuff down, Han?" he asks me.

"Of course," I tell him. "I'm a writer's daughter. I'm programmed to keep a journal. It's genetic."

He laughs and tells me he's been keeping a journal since he was twenty-six years old. "Still have every one of 'em too," he boasts proudly.

I do the math in my head. My dad is forty-two, which means he's been keeping a journal for sixteen years.

"Can I read them?" I ask him, knowing he'll never go for it.

"Sure. If I can read yours." He smiles, looking almost wise.

"Um . . . nah. That's okay," I say. Some things I write are for my eyes only.

"Figured as much," he chuckles.

By nine o'clock, I'm so tired I can barely drag myself up the staircase to my loft. My feet feel like they're made out of cast iron. I flop onto my bed and lie there thinking about the events of the day. I wonder what Cowichan Bay looked like one hundred years ago, when the Native villages were still around: before the mountains were scarred by clear-cuts and the highways had pushed their way through the forest. When there weren't any ferries stinking up the ocean, and zillions of salmon came back each year for their autumn run.

I feel like I got to see a piece of that world today, a hint of another time and place. I go to sleep thinking about silent forests with big, big trees, a ghostly voice and a strange black raven.

12

Raven Magic

꧁

THE FIRST THING I DO when I wake up the next morning is clasp my hands together to stop them from shaking. I reach under my bed for my journal. My fingers feel clumsy, like fat sausages, so it's hard to write fast. I need to get everything down about this dream before I forget.

Wednesday, June 17, 2010
Dear Diary:

I spoke to the Native girl in my dream! I met her in the woods. She was standing right there in front of me. It was so real and I can remember everything. Her face, her clothes, the shocked look on our faces when we each realized that, even though we spoke different languages, we could both totally understand each other. The smell of wood smoke was strong and I could see it curling from a clearing beyond the trees. And the raven — my raven — was sitting on the branch of that same cedar tree, the one just off the trail by the cave. I'm sure it was the same place! He was watching us carefully, and hopping around and fluffing his wings, and he stayed there for the whole dream.

In the dream, I just knew that this girl was from another time. A time way before mine. She told me that she'd been waiting for me, that she'd seen me in her dreams, in the same forest. And just when it was really getting interesting, the raven cawed loudly, flapped his wings, and flew right between us. Then he disappeared high up into the trees. Me and this girl were both trying to figure out where he'd gone. Somehow, we knew that he knew more about what was happening than we did — and then I woke up!

This dream is the most real of all. I remember so many of the teeny details, like the smell of the smoke and the sound of the raven's wings rustling. I especially remember his black beady eyes, the way he stared at me as though he was reading my mind, or maybe the other girl's. There was something about him. My raven. Was Jim right? Does that bird know things I don't? Why am I the one having these weird dreams anyway? I need to know more, especially about ravens.

School drags until Max and I tell everybody where we'd been yesterday, and why we'd been there. No one can believe it, and they ask a ton of questions.

"Well, my dad says that archaeology is just an excuse for the government to spend money it doesn't have," Sabrina Webber says. She's sitting primly at her desk, and she's wearing hot pink lip gloss with silver glitter in it. Gross.

"All I know is that it felt pretty cool to find something that might be two hundred years old," I tell her. I know she's hoping I'll argue with her because Sabrina looks for an argument with anyone who has the time. Aunt Maddie says "little Miss Webber" has anger issues.

Mrs. Elford suggests that Max and I do a report on the excavation for our history class assignment. We look at each other and grin. It's going to be so awesome. And we have some really good photographs to go along with it too. Maybe we can even get Mr. Sullivan to come and speak to our class.

At lunch, I tell Max I'm going to the library to get a jump start on some research, so he goes off to eat with Zach and Nathan. They always share the potato chips, root beer and fruit gummies that their mom puts in their lunches.

The library is quiet. Only Mrs. Mason, the librarian, is there, and she's busy on the computer. She looks up briefly, pushes her glasses higher up on the bridge of her nose and says, "Do you need any help, dear?"

"Ummm. Actually I'm looking for a book on Cowichan

Native legends and folklore." I tell her, having rehearsed this line in my head all morning.

She doesn't hesitate at all, and points to the aisle by the window. "Right at the back, dear — bottom two rows."

"Thanks, Mrs. Mason." I pull off my backpack and set it down near the old radiator by the windowsill.

It isn't long before I find a big hardcover book called *Stories of the Salish Sea.* I flip through it looking for animals and their symbolic meanings, legends, anything to do with ravens. And I find it almost immediately, but when I read what it says, a chill runs through my whole body. This just keeps getting freakier!

> The raven can travel between different worlds, coming and going into the darkest places to bring back visions and instructions for both the seeker and the healer. Ravens are figures of magic and symbolize change. Messages that lie beyond time are nestled in the black wings of the raven, and can be read only by those who are worthy of having the knowledge.

What does this mean? I know my last dream was from a different time. Is my raven really a figure of magic, just like the book says? Is he really flying between space and time? And if he is, what's his reason? What's the message? I have my journal with me, so I copy this information, word for word, onto a page in the back. I finish writing just as the bell rings, and pack away my journal. On my way to class, I can't stop thinking about ravens.

Later on, our class plays a game of volleyball and I suck so badly that even Mr. Ramsey, my P.E. teacher, asks me if I'm feeling okay. I tell him I went to bed really late and that I'm just tired.

Max asks me if I want to hang out after school but I decide that I want to head right home. I haven't seen Nell in a couple days so I want to stop by the bakery.

"But I'll ride the bus with you to your place 'cause I want to walk the trail home." I kind of have an even bigger appreciation for the woods now.

Mr. Bussman is our bus driver. Really. That's his actual name: Buss Man. He seems pretty nice but he never says much. It's barely detectable, but he has a hint of a smile on his face most of the time, as if he's got some private joke going on. I think he has a secret life somewhere else. Anyway, Max and I bet on who can make him crack a real smile first, but we don't have any luck. Mr. Bussman didn't so much as twitch.

"He's made of plastic," Max whispers to me. I stuff my face into my backpack to muffle my laugh, but soon I have to get up because it's our stop.

"See ya kids," Mr. Bussman says as we step down off the bus. "You two sure crack me up." Max and I look at each other and then collapse into a mad laugh attack right there on the side of the road. Once it passes, we go our separate ways.

"See ya, Hannah. Don't forget to upload your pics and email them to me," Max reminds me.

"Okay. See you tomorrow," I call over my shoulder, as I head across the road to the trail.

The air is still and warm, and buzzing insects have appeared out of nowhere these past couple of days. The ground feels kind of springy under my feet as I bounce along the trail, probably because it rained a little in the night.

My stomach growls and I start thinking about dinner. My dad goes to his writing group on Wednesday nights so I'll probably just have a sandwich, even though I'm craving chicken caesar wraps. Dad and I love them, especially the spicy kind. Good thing I plan on stopping at the Toad to see Nell. She always has brownie edges that need to get eaten. I don't even care if they're a little burnt.

Suddenly, I'm not thinking about food anymore. I stop walking and listen. There it is again. "Hannah." My name. Louder now. It's that girl's voice again. Okay, I'm not going crazy; I heard it plain as day. I stand there with my feet rooted to the ground, my body stiff. I don't know whether to run as fast as I can, or stay completely still. First the dreams, and now her voice! Is it because I'm so hungry? Am I light-headed, delirious? I tell myself not to be scared, and I make myself sit on a rock beside the trail. I wait, listening for everything, hearing nothing. Except for the raven. He's back, and he's making that weird call that ravens make . . . blah-doo . . . blah-doo. I always got a kick out of that call. I spend a lot of time in the woods, and it's one noise I can mimic pretty well. The raven's kind of familiar now — my raven — not so strange or scary. I call back to him just for fun. The woods are silent at first, and then he calls again, more intensely than the first time, as if he really is answering me.

We go back and forth for a bit and I start to feel like my old self again. What was I thinking? Hearing voices! It was obviously the raven. They can imitate almost anything. And if Sadie the parrot can say "Kitty-on-a-stick," then why can't a raven say "Hannah?" He was hanging around the cave a lot while we were there. He must have heard my name spoken aloud at least a zillion times. "Yes, that explains it . . . now, don't you feel better?" I stand up, about to continue on my way, and then realize I was just talking to myself. All this thinking about history and legends, together with those crazy dreams, has made me kind of sketchy! What next?

Mom always told me I had enough imagination for two — usually after a bad dream woke me up, when I was a little kid. I remember how she would pad into my room in her woolly hand-knit slippers and whisper, "Uh-oh, Hannah Banana's brain is working overtime again, isn't it!" I cross my arms in front, hug my hoodie close, and continue my walk down the trail. Even though I'm getting closer to home, something just doesn't seem . . . right. It's too quiet, and the light on the trail is unusually misty. Kind of hazy; like looking into a steamy bathroom mirror. I try blinking, but the more I try to focus, the more disoriented I become.

I take a couple of deep breaths. Just as I've decided to stop walking, the mists lift; enough so I can see that I'm right beside a familiar patch of salal. I see the markers left by Mr.

Sullivan and the team, which means I'm only feet from the cave. Even though I'm still anxious, I also feel a pull, a need, to see it again. I argue for and against: it's getting late; this area is now an official dig site; I'm not supposed to disturb anything; I promised Dad I wouldn't go near the cave by myself; and blah, blah, blah . . . I leave the trail and plunge into the thick mass of salal.

My heart is pounding as I reach the rock face. I drop to the ground and squeeze myself in through the cave opening, all in a matter of seconds. I wait for my eyes to adjust to the darkness ahead of me. I inch farther and farther into the damp stillness of the cave, leaving behind the only sliver of light coming from the cave opening. Ugh! It's so dark and I can't stop thinking about Max's creepy skeleton guy.

I inch forward, feeling my way along until I come to the place where I can stand up. Why did I do this? I feel like I'm having a heart attack or something — my pulse is racing and my forehead is beaded with sweat. What's happening to me? What am I doing here, in the dark? I should just go home. But I can't. My feet feel stuck to the ground and I can't move my body. I feel frozen to the spot.

Then I hear it again. Her voice! She's calling me: "HAANNNAAAHH!" Now I know for sure — this is no raven. Fear takes over, and I shout into the darkness, "WHO ARE YOU? WHY ARE YOU CALLING ME?"

Silence. And then the drumming starts. At first faint, then louder and louder. A steady, rhythmic beat that doesn't seem to come from any one direction, but feels more like thunder — shaking the air around me. The eerie forlorn voice calls my name; the drums beat a steady boom, boom, boom; a howling wind whistles through the cave entrance, carrying the smell of . . . smoke! Like in the dream, only this time it really does burn my eyes. I think my chest is going to burst but, as hard as I try, I still can't move! The cave is spinning, or maybe it's me; all is chaos! I squeeze my eyes shut against the stinging wind and when I try to open them, I can't. I can't open my eyes! I can't move! My mind screams: "What's happening to me?" I've never been so afraid in my life.

The drums are faster and louder now, and my body shakes with every beat. The swirling makes me sick and, just when I feel as though my heart is going to jump right out of my body — when I think my legs are going to buckle underneath me — everything stops and all is quiet.

There is nothing but darkness, and the sound of breathing.

13

Tl'ulpalus

❧

THANK GOODNESS THE breathing inside the cave is my own. All else is quiet. I open my eyes — I can open my eyes — and when I rub them, my face feels cold and wet. Did I faint? I shiver and pull my hoodie tight around my body. Then it hits me: I can move again; but my head is foggy and I've lost all track of time. How long have I been in here? Suddenly, all I want to do is get out of this dark hole and go home. It's gotten way too intense for me, too intense to handle alone. Enough is enough!

Inching along, back to the opening of the cave, I am desperate to see the light. When I reach the rock face, there's still no light. The light is gone. Which means the opening is gone. I sweep the flat of my hands back and forth across the rock surface, frantically searching near the ground, but it isn't there. I try not to lose it altogether; I tell myself that I'm just confused by everything that's happened. I need to relax and get my bearings. I force myself to breathe deeply and slowly, just like Aunt Maddie taught me, and search again. But it's no good. The opening is gone.

Don't panic! Whatever you do, don't panic. I know if I panic, I won't get anywhere, so I slowly and carefully start inching my way along in the opposite direction, hoping desperately for a sliver of light, no matter how small. And just as I feel the hot prickle of a tear sliding down the side of my cheek, I see it. A shaft of watery light coming from around a bend.

I'm too grateful to be cautious, and within seconds I see an opening. A different opening, but, at least, an opening. It's a long narrow gap in the rock, and I have to stand sideways and suck in my stomach as much as I can in order to squeeze through it.

While I'm relieved finally to be outside, in the light, breathing fresh air, I'm completely disoriented. Where am I? I recognize the woods, but where's the trail? And why is it so quiet? I can't hear any of the usual noise from the road that goes past the marina, only the sounds of the forest all around me. The trees are taller and wider, and the light is fighting to break through the thick green canopy overhead. Huge sword ferns and tangles of bramble vines surround me in all directions. I check my digital watch. It isn't working. I tap it a couple of times with my fingernail, but it seems to be stuck at 4:11:26 p.m. That's weird; it feels like morning. The light is pale and new, and I can hear shore birds in the distance now, calling over the sound of the ocean. How long was I in the cave? I walk around, testing a few steps, on legs stiff from being frozen in the same position for what felt like an eternity. When was that?

I see a tangle of blackberry vines with ripe — and I mean *ripe* — blackberries, a few feet away. My stomach growls and I realize that I'm hungry, so I go over and stuff my mouth with berries. The juice is delicious and sweet and my fingers instantly stain a dark purple. Blackberries? I stop eating as it hits me. You don't get blackberries in June. Blackberries are in August. I always go blackberry picking just before school starts up again. Whoa . . . just how long has my watch been stopped?

I look around again to get my bearings. It usually only takes five more minutes to get from here to the road that crosses to Nell's bakery. Somehow I know that isn't the case anymore. There isn't any trail, and I can't see or hear any road. And if there isn't any road, then there isn't any bakery, which means there isn't any Nell. If there isn't any Nell, then — worst of all — there isn't any Dad. There isn't any . . . anybody!

It takes a moment to sink in. But, if that's true . . . it means I'm alone.

"*Uy' skweyul.*"

I whirl around, adrenaline surging through my body. "What . . . who's there?" I call out to no one in particular.

Silence. And then I see her, a girl about my age. She's standing only fifteen feet away from me. Her arms rest by her sides and she's staring straight at me. Even though she looks scared, I recognize her immediately. It's the girl in my dreams.

"Who are you?" I ask, but she seems confused and doesn't answer. Instead she looks nervously behind her and then steps to one side to peer behind me. I turn to look. There's nothing there. Just tall, tall trees and a whole lot of quiet. I turn back to face her.

"Your name?" I try again. "What's your name?" I point to her and try to make my face look like I'm asking a question. I raise my eyebrows. She just keeps looking around, as if she's expecting someone, or something. Sure enough, a big black raven appears and perches on a rock beside her. It's my raven! I'd recognize him anywhere, even here. He cackles, a low raspy call, and the girl's eyes light up. She nods, suddenly able to understand my question.

"Yisella," she says quickly, watching me nervously, and then turns back to the raven.

"Yis . . . what?" I ask, hoping she'll repeat it.

"Yisella," she says again, patting her chest, her eyes darting anxiously in all directions. Now what is she looking for?

"Yisella," I say slowly. She nods and then she points to me hurriedly.

"Oh, right. I'm Hannah. My name is Hannah."

Yisella looks to the raven and he turns his head to one side and makes a funny soft trilling noise.

"Okay. I thought so. Hannah," she repeats.

Yisella is thin. Too thin, I think. Her hair is straight and dark, hanging down her back. Her eyes are also dark, and deep set, and she wears a knee-length skirt made from some sort of shredded bark. It looks heavy and warm. A luminous turquoise and silver crescent of abalone shell hangs from a thin leather cord around her neck. It shines against her brown skin. I recognize the pendant from my dream.

She takes a few steps in my direction, her eyes fixed on mine the whole time. I want to ask her so many things! Where am I? Where is the traffic? Where is my family? Who is she? Why have I been dreaming about her? It is all so impossible, I can't find the words.

Without warning, a loud snap shakes me out of my mental fog. Before I even look in the direction of the sound, Yisella grabs my arm and yanks me sharply after her.

"Come on!" She says — in perfect English.

Soon we're racing across the ground cover, around bushes, under cedar boughs. There's no time to ask why we're running or where we're going or how this strange girl can now speak my language. Yisella doesn't notice that I'm tripping and stumbling, or that my face is getting scratched by the blackberry bushes she's dragging me through.

"Hey!" I protest. If this is another dream, I want to wake up now.

Then, just as suddenly as we began running, we stop, and Yisella lets go of my arm. As I massage my wrist, I'm thinking that this girl may be skinny, but she's strong.

"Why did you —" I start.

"Shhhhhh!" Yisella cuts me off, holding her hand up as if she's halting a speeding train.

So, I don't say anything. I just stand there, my face stinging from the thorns and my feet soggy from the mud. I watch this strange girl turn slowly in a circle, her eyes fixed on the trees that surround us.

"What are you looking for?" I whisper. When she doesn't answer, I give up and look through the trees as well. And that's when I see it. A tall shadowy figure stands about twenty feet away from us. It's huge! It moves silently through the space between two fir trees and then retreats farther into the woods, until it disappears altogether.

I gasp. Yisella slaps her hand over my mouth but I shake it away. "Did you see that? Was that a giant bear or what?"

"No," Yisella says, "not a bear."

"Then, what?"

Whatever it was, Yisella is clearly relieved that it's gone. She takes a big slow breath, and then she comes and stands in front of me and touches my shoulder.

"*Hwunitum.*"

"*Hwuni*-what?"

"*Hwunitum.* White man," she says.

"White man? Wait a second. How can you speak English? How do you know all these words?"

She smiles and points to the raven. He's perched on the rock, his head turning from Yisella and then to me, as we speak. Is it true? Is he really the trickster, a messenger of magic? Strangely — but then everything here is strange — I'm not afraid. I feel as though I've been waiting to be in this very spot for a long time. In a funny sort of way, as if I'm meant to be here. How crazy does that sound? Maybe Aunt Maddie was right when she said I'm not eating right and should be taking more B vitamins.

I stare back at this girl, at Yisella, and it's nuts because I feel as though I know her. She's so familiar to me. And then she looks at my mud-streaked orange hoodie and my backpack and my dumb black-and-white basketball sneakers, and raises her eyebrows. It's pretty obvious that I am as foreign to her as she is to me.

She turns to go, beckoning me to follow her. There is no trail, so we pick our way through the bracken fern and undergrowth — this time there's no crazy running through the bushes. Walking along, I see that her feet are wrapped in what looks like cedar bark, and they are quick and quiet on the forest floor. I'm like some clumsy elephant behind her, the way the twigs snap and crack beneath my feet.

"Yisella? Where are we going?" I ask, as she follows the raven who flies in front, just above her head.

"Back to my village. I was only out here because of you, waiting for you to come. I had a feeling it might be today."

"You've been waiting for me? How do you even know me?"

"I had so many dreams, and I could see your home. It sits

on top of the water, right?" Yisella says this matter-of-factly, as though this is not unusual. I'm speechless. She looks at me, expecting me to say something. But my tongue feels tied up in a thousand knots, so I don't say anything. I just stare at the coil of smoke I see rising above the trees behind her.

"Come on," she says, taking hold of my sleeve. "My village is really close now."

"Your village?

"Tl'ulpalus. My village."

"Tl'ulpalus!" That's the name of your village — Tl'ulpalus?" I get chills on the back of my neck. Tl'ulpalus is the name of the village that was near my home long ago. I remember Mr. Sullivan telling us, the day we were at the dig site, that it used to be "just a stone's throw away" from my houseboat. Which means . . . this is Cowichan Bay! I'm starting to think that anything is possible now. In the blink of an eye, everything I ever believed about time and space has changed and I have so many questions.

"Yes. Tl'ulpalus," she replies, "our home. Soon we will cross the water one more time to trade and then return again."

I have no choice but to follow her.

We step through the last stand of trees and arrive at the edge of Yisella's village. I stop walking and just stand there and stare. It's all so familiar, this Tl'ulpalus: the curve of the bay, the towering trees, the ocean birds circling above our heads.

I see a row of large plank longhouses, each of them facing out to the bay, their doorways facing the ocean. Massive carved figures stand on either side of the entrances. A couple of the houses have gentle plumes of smoke coiling up through openings in different parts of the roofs, and you can hear an occasional snap or a pop from the firepits that burn inside. I remember the longhouse at the museum in Victoria — how I like to go inside and just sit, not really thinking about anything. This looks kind of the same, only the houses here are way more weather-beaten, kind of a sea-bleached grey.

People are scattered throughout the village. Most, if not all, appear to be busy doing something. An older man squats nearby, carving large curls of bark from a big cedar log lying on the ground. He's frowning slightly at the scraping tool in his hands — and he is naked! He sees Yisella and smiles, but when he sees me, his smile disappears. I smile anyway, even though I feel totally awkward.

Most of the people in the village are wearing clothing, but a few of the older people are like this man: completely naked. The only other naked old people I've ever seen were on Hornby Island. I saw them playing badminton on a little beach last summer when Dad and I paddled past them in our kayak. To be honest, they kind of grossed me out.

Several children race in and out of the houses, shouting and laughing, and running away from an older kid, about sixteen, who roars like a bear and chases them into the woods on the other side of the village. Their laughter echoes above the treetops for a long time.

But it's a woman seated outside one of the longhouses that

holds my attention. She, too, is wearing a fringed skirt of shredded cedar bark, like Yisella's, and she has a grey wool blanket with a red stripe draped around her shoulders. The blanket looks a lot like the one my dad has in the back of our Jeep. With long sweeping strokes, the woman combs through the hair of a young girl seated in front of her. The girl is playing with something in her lap. At first I think that it's a doll or a toy but when it wriggles, I realize that it's a small grey cat.

The woman raises her head to scan the beach, and I see that her eyes are soft and kind. Her manner is gentle, somehow familiar. I feel my throat begin to tighten and my eyes begin to sting, just like they did when I saw Max's mom brushing his sister's hair while they sat outside on the front step. My heart is filled with emotion and my thoughts are flooded with memories.

But I shake it off. The last thing I need right now is to be reminded of Mom. I need to be clearheaded and to stay grounded. I need to focus on the here and now, because there's way more going on than I can understand and now I need to find out why.

14
Hannah's Gift

❧

"YISELLA!" THE WOMAN stops combing the girl's hair and looks straight at us. Yisella quits watching the little kids playing in the woods and turns to her. The woman motions for her to come, but Yisella just sighs and seems irritated. I'm pretty sure that this woman is her mother. I can tell Yisella doesn't really want to go, but she does, and I dutifully follow, trying my best to ignore the wide-eyed stares from the villagers as we walk by. They're looking at me as if I'm some kind of freak. Pointing at my hair and stuff. Okay . . . that's kind of normal.

The raven hops along beside us, his beady eyes watching

our every move. I smile my best Walt-Disney-Perfect-Child smile, hoping it's enough, and tentatively reach behind to the pocket of my backpack, feeling for my iPod. What would they think of this? What would Yisella think of the 3,047 songs that I have on it? Stuff by Feist, Nickelback, Beyoncé and the Black Eyed Peas? How do I explain downloading? The internet? Cell phones?

My mind is awhirl again, but I quickly snap out of it when we reach Yisella's mother. Now that we're close, I see that the girl with the cat is a little older than Yisella, maybe fourteen? Like Yisella, she has the same inky black hair that reaches all the way down her back. Her eyes, too, are dark and clear, and she stares at me without blinking, which makes me feel totally awkward — that is, even more awkward than I was already. I smile at her and try to look cheerful.

"Hi," I chirp, trying to sound confident but my voice comes out way higher than usual, with a little catch in it.

Yisella and her mother talk in hushed tones and, although they speak in a language that is completely unfamiliar to me, I hear my name in there a couple of times. What are they saying about me? That I just teleported through time? That I just dropped in from the year 2010 for a casual visit and a cup of tea? Yisella's mother seems to relax a little; the tension in her face recedes, especially when Yisella points to the raven sitting on a post, just a little ways off. Yisella smiles and looks at me. "My mother wants you to know their names. She is Skeepla and my older sister is Nutsa. She's the number one daughter. Nutsa means number one in our language and Yisella means number two. I'm the number two daughter."

I nod my understanding and smile at them both until Skeepla sort of smiles back at me, but it's not exactly a real smile. It's the fake kind that teachers always give your parents on meet-the-creature-night at school. Nutsa glares at me — I am definitely not welcome — while they both check out my clothes. What I'm wearing must look really bizarre to them. I doubt if they've ever seen jeans or an orange Quicksilver hoodie before. They seem especially curious about my green and black checkered backpack, which reminds me that not only is my iPod inside it but so is my digital camera. I barely hesitate before I reach inside and fish around for it. I find it hidden inside Max's baseball hat, although I don't know how that ended up in my backpack. I remove the camera and hit the power button.

"It's for taking pictures," I tell Yisella, who looks suspiciously at the bright red Coolpix camera I'm holding in front of her. "Never mind. Look. I'll show you how it works."

I feel sort of stupid bringing out my camera but I haven't got any better ideas, so I back up a little bit and focus it, making sure that I have Yisella, Nutsa, and Skeepla all displayed in the viewfinder. The three of them look at each other before taking a few tentative steps backwards. Maybe they think the camera is some kind of weapon or something. Then I take the shot and the flash goes off. Startled, they look as if they're about to make a run for it.

"No, No . . . it's all right. Really. Look!" I say.

No one comes forward, but at least they're still here. All stare wide-eyed at my camera, not knowing what to think. But, after a bit, and when nothing horrible happens, Yisella approaches to see what I've done. A big smile breaks out over her face when she sees the photograph, and she hops up and down waving for her mother and sister to come over and have a look.

They are all fascinated and pass the camera back and forth between them, pointing at each other and laughing. Maybe I'm not so stupid after all. This was the best idea ever. They've forgotten all about my strange clothes and my wild hair. Skeepla's smile is the real deal now and her eyes are bright with wonder. I show her how to focus the camera, how to find the subject in the viewfinder and how to zoom in.

She wants me to do it over and over again until, finally, she motions for me to stand in front of her so that she can push the button herself. We look at the picture together and, even though I'm smiling, I look seriously uptight. Nervous. Which isn't all that weird because I'm pretty sure this is not a dream, which means that I've just travelled back in time about a hundred years or so. Who wouldn't be nervous?

I take some more photos and then put the camera away even though everyone is still pretty excited about it. They're all laughing until Yisella and Nutsa lock eyes. Instantly, the smile disappears from my new friend's face and what could only be a scowl takes its place. Nutsa sees it too and drops her eyes to the ground, but I can see that she's smirking from behind her hair, as though she's gotten away with something. Nobody says anything. I don't even try to figure this one out. Maybe it's just a sister thing. Like the way my friend Gwyneth used to be with her sister Julie. They used to fight all the time, and sometimes their arguments were so stupid. Over stuff like exfoliating face wash, or who got a bigger piece of cheesecake.

Yisella then takes me into one of the longhouses. As soon as we push aside the animal hide hanging in the doorway and step through, I'm hit with a million different sights and smells. There's stuff like skins and fish hanging from the ceiling, and shelves full of tools, baskets and boxes all over the walls. Smoke is the most obvious smell, but there's another one — a warm sweet delicious smell that I can't quite identify. I see another rack of dried fish on the other side of the room against the far wall, and I figure that's got to be it. Is it salmon? As if she knows exactly what I'm thinking, Yisella walks over to one of the racks, breaks off a piece of fish, and brings it back to me.

"Here. Have some," she urges. "You're hungry, right?" She pushes the fish into my hand and it's only then that my hunger returns. I'm actually starving. I can't remember when I last ate, except for the blackberries, which don't count. In all the excitement, I forgot how hungry and how tired I am. The fish tastes delicious. Sweet and moist, but dry enough that small flakes tear away easily. It's like nothing I've ever tasted before and I finish it quickly. I look up and see Yisella smiling at me. I must look like a half-starved lunatic, but I figure that is exactly what I might be — a lunatic.

As I'm licking my fingertips, thinking about how I could easily eat another twelve pieces of the smoked salmon, Nutsa walks through the door. The little grey cat follows right behind her. Yisella's eyes narrow and grow cold again. She watches as her sister walks, unhurriedly, over to a raised platform covered with a woven cedar bark blanket and furry animal pelt, and flops herself down on top. Obviously, it is where she sleeps. The cat jumps up and nestles in next to her. It has a little diamond-shaped patch of white fur between its eyes. Seeing it curled up next to Nutsa makes me miss Chuck. Yisella sighs, drumming her fingertips against her leg, and stares up at the smoke hole in the ceiling.

"Nutsa!" she says loudly, both hands now straight and rigid at her sides. Nutsa turns her head slowly in the direction of her sister's voice. Yisella then begins to speak, quickly and angrily, foreign words that I don't understand. But I can tell from her tone that she's pretty angry and that Nutsa is sure getting into trouble for something!

Nutsa doesn't answer. She just looks bored and impatient, the way most of the kids look when Mrs. Elford starts talking about fractions in math class. She waits for her sister to finish talking, and then slowly gets up off her mat and wanders outside, as though she doesn't have a care in the world. The cat stays behind to sleep where it is safe.

I must look puzzled, because Yisella turns to me and says

angrily, "Nutsa is such a lazy girl! She's the older daughter! There are things she has to do but she never does! She just waits for everyone else to do her work for her. I'm so sick of her lazy ways. She should know better! She'll never have a blanketing ceremony if she doesn't change. She disgraces our whole family. And she's over fourteen summers old. She'll never have a husband. Who would want such a lazy wife!"

Yisella sits down on the floor of the longhouse and drags a stick mindlessly across the hard-packed earth. I don't say anything, mainly because I'm just not sure what to say. There's no way I'm going to get involved in some kind of family dispute. That would be a dumb idea and I can't afford to make any enemies here. Besides, I never say anything bad about people I don't even know. That's just low.

We sit there for a moment, each of us silent and a little bit shy, more aware now that we don't really know the first thing about each other.

She looks up at me and then over to the corner of the longhouse. "Nutsa was supposed to help my mother with the wool. She was supposed to get the fleece ready to spin. But, no, she goes to the beach and dreams of foolish things! Then she tells Mother silly stories that don't have any meaning. She just sits there while Mother brushes her hair!"

"Is your mother mad at her too," I finally ask, "because she doesn't help?"

"I think it bothers her," Yisella sighs, "but Nutsa won't change."

"Well, you can't make a person do something they don't

want to do." I'm thinking about my own mother's failed attempts to get me to take flute lessons even though she knew that the sound of that instrument made me want to chew my leg off.

Yisella looks at me as though I slapped her. Her mouth opens a bit and her eyes widen with disbelief, but a moment later, she softens and says, "You don't understand, Hannah. My mother is the finest weaver in all Quw'utsun'. Everyone knows her and everyone respects her. Her blankets are better than all the rest. Even over the water, they know of her. Mother's blankets are highly prized gifts and everybody wants one. Nutsa, as the number one daughter, is supposed to help. She disgraces our village because she doesn't care about our mother's gift."

"Why don't you help your mother then?" I ask. It seems like a pretty simple solution.

"Me? I can't. I just don't have the spinning gift."

"Really? How do you know?" I say. "How many times have you tried?"

"Not very many."

"Then how can you know?" I protest. "Honestly, you can't say you're bad at something if you've never really given it a good try. I used to say that about drawing . . . but I never really practised all that much. And now that I do, well, I don't think I'm as good as my friend, Max, but I'm getting way better."

"I know," Yisella explains, twisting the iridescent shell on the cord around her neck with her fingers. "But when you're born, you're born with a gift. My gift is plant medicine, not spinning. That is Nutsa's and my mother's gift. Nutsa just doesn't care. She won't listen. It's a shameful way for her to act. I'm sorry sometimes to call her my sister."

Ouch. Harsh.

Yisella seems close to tears and I can feel her frustration. I reach out and touch her shoulder. She gives me a weak smile, then stands up and brushes her hands off on the front of her skirt.

"Anyway," she says a little more cheerfully, "it isn't my problem to fix. Mother will spin and make her blankets and they will be beautiful with or without Nutsa's help. It's just that she seems so tired the past few days. She just wants to sleep. It's not like her." Yisella again glances over to the corner of the longhouse. My eyes follow her gaze to the many cedar baskets full of grey, brown, or white fluffy fleece, and to the big loom sitting next to the baskets. A stump, draped with a cedar mat, also sits nearby. It must be where Yisella's mother sits when she spins and weaves. I walk over to kind of snoop around and then I notice this dark shape leaning against the biggest basket. I look closer and my breath catches in my throat. I can feel the goosebumps popping up all over my arms, and Yisella raises her eyebrows in a questioning way.

"What's wrong?" she asks, now following my gaze to the object leaning against the basket. I point to it. It's a spindle whorl. My spindle whorl! The same one I found hidden in the cave near the marina. It's not as worn, but I recognize the salmon carved into the wood around the hole in the centre. It has to be the same one!

"That belongs to my mother," says Yisella, "her most prized possession. It was carved especially for her three winters ago." She holds it in her hands, gesturing for me to take it from her. The familiar weight of it is overwhelming: the smoothness of the rich warm-coloured wood; the carved fish with their dancing tail fins, identical to what I remember, only sharper and not yet ravaged by time. I stare into the centre, through the hole, to the fire burning on the other side.

The acrid smoke stings my eyes, but I can't blink, I can't shift my gaze. I try to back away from the smoky pit fire, only my legs are rooted to the ground. Oh, no, it's happening again, just like in the cave.

My hands grip the spindle whorl, as if they are glued to it. Then I see it start to spin. Is it an optical illusion? It has to be, because my hands aren't moving; they feel stuck. I see the images of the fish begin to blur and run together as the disc spins faster and faster before my eyes. I feel light as a feather, even though my heart races a mile a minute and my fingertips are pins and needles. I am powerless, yet at the same time, totally dialled in.

"HANNAH?" Yisella's voice breaks the spell. I look up and see her staring at me, her eyes wide as saucers. I reach up with a free hand to wipe the beads of perspiration from my forehead. I'm actually sweating, as if I had been running on the track at school. The whorl is still in my hand and the smooth wood feels warmer to the touch, almost hot.

"Hannah?" Yisella says again. I look at her, slightly dazed. "Hannah . . . I think you have it. The gift, I mean. I have to tell my mother. She'll want to know about this."

"Yisella," I start, my hands clutching the whorl close to me. My mind is racing with a million different thoughts. This is the same whorl! This has to have something to do with why I'm here. "I've seen this before! Your mother's spindle whorl. I found it in a cave, just a couple of days ago. I mean . . . I'm going to find it in the future, in about one hundred and fifty years. No, I mean . . ." I realize that I am babbling, but I can't stop. Yisella's eyes open wider and wider as I try to explain. "I found it and I showed it to a man who told me that it belonged to the people who lived near my home. People who lived here before the *huww . . . hu . . .* what's that word again? The word for white people?" My heart is pounding in my chest.

"*Hwunitum,*" Yisella says, pronouncing the word clearly for me.

"Yes! The man was talking about your people, Yisella!" I'm trembling now, because at last some pieces of this crazy puzzle are starting to fit together.

"Who is this man?"

"His name is Graham Sullivan. He studies the past. He . . . he told me stuff about your people, about the villages here.

He told me some stories. There was one about Quamichan, a woman with a snake basket. About how . . ."

"Yes!" Yisella suddenly starts gesturing wildly with her hands. "Quamichan! We tell that story! She will steal children from villages and eat them! She has wings and she can fly from the islands out there in the ocean, over here to Quw'utsun'!"

"Yeah! That's the one. So . . . do you see?"

I place the whorl gently on the mat in front of me. "I think I was meant to find this in that cave — so it could bring me to you. I'm sure of it now. Even he was there when I found it!" I point to the raven perched on the corner of the loom. His wings are outstretched, as if he's about to take off.

"Yes," Yisella nods. She is watching him, too, with an odd expression on her face.

"Why do you think this has happened?" I ask her.

"I don't know," she answers. "But I'm happy that it did."

15
Yisella's Ice Cream

꘎

A FEW HOURS LATER, we are still in the longhouse, now sitting together with Yisella's extended family. There sure are a lot of them! Yisella tells me that many people share the longhouse and that four generations live together in her house. I can't imagine that ever working with my family. Having all of our crazy relatives living under one roof? I'm pretty sure we'd all go nuts inside of a week. Especially my dad and my Uncle Barry. There hasn't been a family dinner yet when those two haven't argued about something. The last time was Grandma's birthday dinner, when they fought about some old Clint Eastwood movie.

But here, in Tl'ulpalus, I guess there isn't a choice. And nobody even gets their own room. There's Skeepla and Nutsa and Yisella's father, Squwam. There are also two uncles and three aunties, eight cousins, Skeepla's mother, both of Squwam's parents, and finally Yisella's great-grandmother. Somehow, the longhouse doesn't feel so big anymore!

I think of Dad at home in our puny little houseboat. Is he worried about me? Does he know I'm gone? My watch still says 4:11:26 in the afternoon. It hasn't moved since I got here. None of this makes any sense at all, and I don't seem to have any control over what comes next. I'll just have to wait it out and go with the flow, which isn't really me at all. I'm not very good at just sitting around, waiting for stuff to happen. Life's boring that way. But here? Right now? It's not like I really have any other options.

When Yisella introduces me to the rest of her family, they seem as uncertain of me as her mother and Nutsa were earlier. They don't say anything, just stare at me for what seems like hours, checking me out from head to toe and then back again. It's bad enough when Sabrina Webber gives me that look, but try getting that same look from over fifteen people at once.

Yisella waits while I say my name. I forget that she's the only one who can understand me here and so I keep talking. I go on to explain how I'm this new friend of Yisella's and that I came here from another time. Then I see how confused they all look, so I stop. When Yisella whispers to me that the magic brought by the raven is only for the two of us, I shut up. Duh.

Yisella's grandmother steps forward, her eyes bright and alert. When she smiles, I see that she has a tooth missing. She touches my hair and says something to me that, of course, I don't understand. But I get the feeling that she just made a joke because some of the others cover their mouths to hide their laughter. I know my hair is pretty crazy looking. Why wouldn't they laugh the first time they saw red corkscrew curls like mine? Gwyneth used to say my hair ended up like this because I stuck my finger in a light socket when I was little. That could be true, but I'm sure my hair would have ended up this way anyway. Mom always said it was ridiculous, that my hair had a mind of its own. So I guess when you add in my freckles and my pale skin, I definitely stand out.

Yisella's family all start speaking at once, so I look to Yisella hoping she'll step in if necessary and rescue me. She says that everyone is a little weirded out by me. They don't really know any white people, except for the occasional trader who comes to the village from time to time for furs.

There was one other time when a group of white men came to Tl'ulpalus and spoke in angry voices to her people. No one knew why these men were angry, but it had something to do with Quw'utsun', the land that they live on. She tells me that those men wanted to grow their own food on this land, even though the *hwunitum* stay with their own families much farther up near the flats.

"But you . . ." she says. "No one in our village has ever seen a *hwunitum* child. And . . . well, they think you're very skinny and pale." She giggles.

What did I tell you? Well, they can stare all they want. I'm just grateful that I won't have to listen to any "ginger" jokes.

Two of the littlest cousins keep coming up to me and touching my hair, then they run away laughing and whispering to each other, making it some sort of game. The third time that they get close, I reach out and tickle the smallest one, a little boy with fat smiling cheeks and black hair falling in front of his eyes. He collapses into my lap, laughing and squealing with excitement. Why is it that little kids are never as suspicious as grown-ups are? These little kids couldn't care less that I'm different. In a second, the other little guy jumps on me as well, and they both dissolve into fits of giggles. The same little boy fiddles with the zipper on my backpack, and it's not long before he discovers my lime green iPod Nano. He turns it over and over in his hands and, in no time at all, everybody else is gathered around him, straining to get a better look. Yisella pushes through the crowd and takes the iPod from the little boy.

"What is this?" she asks me, uncurling the tangle of earbuds plugged into the top. How am I going to explain this? I think for a minute, then I remember what my dad always says. Show, don't tell. Dad says it's the most important rule for a writer to obey — okay, so it's a writer thing. I stand up and carefully put the earbuds into Yisella's ears. She doesn't try to take them out, but just stands there patiently, not moving a muscle. I take the iPod out of her hand and scroll through my main playlist. I decide on "Yellow" by Coldplay, set the volume, and then watch as the biggest smile I've seen yet from Yisella spreads across her face. Everyone wants to try and it's hard work organizing a turn for each one of them. They talk excitedly, one to another, and hold their hands over their ears. The little kids jump around in circles. One of the older men looks completely muddled but he still nods his head in time with the music. I can't help laughing to myself as I watch him. Eventually I'm able to turn it off and put it away.

With the iPod back in my backpack, the children decide that it's time to chase the little grey cat, or "Poos" as the villagers call it. We all sit down once again on the floor of the longhouse, and I'm relieved to see that pretty much everyone is more at ease with me now.

Soon everyone is busy with something. I'm not sure what to do next, so I decide to, literally, twiddle my thumbs. When Yisella points to a bowl on the mat next to where I'm sitting, I reach down and hand it to her. It's a shallow burnished dish made from a maple tree burl. I recognize the dark and grainy wood that's often used to make clocks and stuff, like the ones I've seen in souvenir stores. Moments later, Yisella hands it back, only now it's filled with a wonderful sweet-smelling concoction, made of what looks like dried black-berries, topped with frothy pink creamy stuff. Even though

I'm not exactly showing the best table manners, I scoop some up with the end of my finger and then lick it off. It's surprisingly delicious and kind of like whipped cream! I wonder how they make it? There's no ice cream here or frozen yogurt. There aren't any refrigerators or freezers, and no way are there any chocolate bars or candies.

When Yisella looks over, I smile and lick my lips, pointing at my bowl. She laughs and says, "That's *sxhwesum* berry. Tiny berries that turn into a big frothy foam when they are stirred over and over. We make it for our special celebrations. The children love it the most, especially now that the *hwunitum* are here."

"*Hwunitum*. The white people? Why?" I ask, wondering how their arrival into the wilds of the island could make this treat taste any more delicious!

"The *hwunitum* sometimes bring us sugar. We give them rabbit pelts and they give us sacks of sugar. The sugar mixed with *sxhwesum* berry is especially good!"

"Ohhhh!" Now I understand, and agree. "Yeah, sugar's the best! I know someone who bakes a lot of delicious stuff with sugar and flour."

"Yes, flour too! Flour and sugar," Yisella says enthusiastically. "We trade rabbit pelts for both of these things. A while ago, a white woman showed my auntie how to make bannock bread."

I remembered that my dad made some bannock bread in a heavy cast-iron frying pan over an open fire when we went camping last summer. We poured blueberry syrup all over the warm slabs of bread, and ate about ten pieces each for dinner.

Now that everyone has finished the meal, they gather and sit quietly around a big fire in the corner fire pit, waiting expectantly. The older women settle the smaller children, shushing them while taking the littlest ones onto their laps. I watch as Yisella places a woven cedar mat onto the ground near her mother.

"Yisella," I whisper, "what's happening? Why is everyone sitting in a circle?" I sit on the ground next to Yisella, together with Nutsa and their mother, Skeepla, on the cedar mat.

"It's time for the *Nahnum*, the fire circle." She explains, "Usually we do this in wintertime, but you are my guest, our guest, and so today is special. The *Nahnum* is when the elders teach us things and we get to hear stories of the old times. It is good for us to have the *Nahnum* now, just before we leave."

"Leave?" I say. "You're going somewhere?"

"Oh," Yisella laughs. "We'll leave again very soon. Summer is the busiest time, when we make trips across the water to trade with the river people. We only come back to Tl'ulpalus long enough to get ready for the next trip across — in summer that is. And this will be our last trip this summer. During winter we stay here all the time."

"What do you trade for?" I ask. It seems like things are backwards here. I always thought summer was for sleeping late, for lying around watching DVDs, or hanging out with friends and swimming at the beach.

"We give them salmon and they give us other things, but the best thing is the goat's wool we use to weave blankets. The river people can only collect wool in the springtime, when the mountain goats leave their fleece on the trees and bushes. So we go in the summertime to get as much as we can. It's the most important trip for Mother."

Blankets made of goat hair? I think of my cashmere sweater, the one that Aunt Maddie bought for me last Christmas. It's softer than anything. I can't imagine what kind of a sweater you could possibly make from a goat! And what about those dogs that Mr. Sullivan said were used for their woolly coats? I ask Yisella about them.

"Oh, I've never seen them," she tells me. "That was before I was born, but Grandmother remembers. There were lots of them then, in the villages up the river, but they aren't around anymore."

"We have wool too," I tell Yisella. "But it comes from sheep and it comes in all different colours. My mother was a really amazing knitter!" I do my best to ignore the lump forming in my throat, the lump that comes out of nowhere every single time I talk or even think about my mother.

"Knitting?" Yisella is confused for a moment, but then she seems to understand. "With the two sticks, right? You work them together on your lap. There was a white woman who came with the man that wanted otter pelts, and she showed

Mother how to weave with the sticks. It's very fast and the weaving is even."

"Yeah, they're called knitting needles. Different sizes make different sized stitches. I was just learning how to knit, when my——" I stop.

"You said your mother was a knitter. Doesn't she knit anymore?" Yisella asks, somewhat puzzled.

It's so hard to answer questions like this one. Questions that mean I will have to explain. I say the words, "My mother is dead," and it sounds like someone else talking, so matter-of-factly, like "it's raining," or "the earth is round." But I say the words to Yisella anyway.

"She died in——" and then I realize that Yisella won't know what I mean when I tell her my mother died in a car accident. There are no cars here, so I just say, "She died in an accident. It was almost two years ago."

Yisella's eyes lock with mine for a moment while I struggle with my emotions. She doesn't say anything, but I can tell that she understands about "the lump." I'm grateful when she doesn't ask me any more questions, because I'm pretty sure that if she did, I wouldn't be able to say anything. Not now, not here, where everything seems like a dream and I'm not sure when, or even if, I'm going to wake up. While everyone is very accepting of me, I am still an outsider, and it's times like this when I feel unsure of myself and get confused, that I really miss my mom. She could always calm me down. Dad can make me laugh most of the time when I get bummed out or mad, but it was always Mom who could put things into proper perspective for me. She made everything make sense.

I feel like I'm drowning in the memories, and I'm going to be swallowed up by them. Instead, I am surrounded with a strong smell of lemons that seems to come out of nowhere. Just like that, a fresh citrus scent fills my senses, but only for a moment before it dissipates as quickly as it came. I smile because I know what — or should I say *who* — it was. There are no lemons here; no fruit like that anywhere in Tl'ulpalus. I'd almost forgotten about Mom's lemon fragrance. How she would always dab it on my wrists if I was nervous about something I had to do and she couldn't be with me. "There you go," she'd say. "Because I can't be with you today, this is second best." And I remember how the lemony scent alone would make me feel stronger. How could I have forgotten something so special about Mom?

I don't say anything to Yisella, but deep in my heart I know it was Mom, here, wearing her lemon fragrance just as she always did. I know it was her way of letting me know that she's with me, on this crazy adventure, or in this dream, or whatever this experience is. And although the smell is gone, the memory of it stays with me for a long time.

It's enough to make me feel safe and so much calmer now, as I sit here on the mat waiting with Yisella and the others. Yisella looks at me kindly, knowing that my uncomfortable moment has passed and I'm pretty much okay again.

Then I catch Nutsa staring at me, and when our eyes meet, I notice that hers are icy cold and unblinking. I look away first, and notice Yisella watching her mother's movements, the way she sighs and rubs her back with the palm of her hands. I recall what Yisella said earlier about how hard and how long her mother works.

Slivers of early evening's sunlight stream through the spaces between several planks in the longhouse walls. It is warm and golden and it makes me think of summer evenings back home. By now, I'd probably have finished dinner and be outside with Chuck on the deck, watching for the one-eyed seal that's been coming around our houseboat for almost a year now. My dad still calls him "One-Eye," even though I told him it was a pretty lame and unimaginative name for a writer to come up with.

There would be sounds of laughter and clinking dishes coming from the patio of the Salty Dog Café up near the road, and Nell's dog, Quincy, would be hanging around outside the back door waiting for the leftover fish and chip scraps. But I'm not there, I'm here. At the *Nahnum*, my first fire circle. And the air is electric.

16
Nahnum

❧

ALL IS QUIET, EVEN the little ones, as a very old woman, Yisella's great-grandmother, stands and walks slowly over to sit near the fire. She is small and bent, and her pure white hair is pulled into a single tight braid that follows the length of her spine. Although her face is weathered and lined with age, her eyes are alert as they shine brightly in the firelight. She nods and gives one of the little children sitting closest to her a wide toothless smile.

She wears a skirt made of the same stringy material as the mats we sit on, only it is finer and softer in the way it hangs around her legs. She pats her lap and Poos, the cat, nestles in for a nap. He covers his face with his paws.

Abruptly, great-grandmother begins to speak. Quietly at first, almost in a whisper, but then her voice grows louder and her words more clipped, coming quickly now. Her eyes grow wider and wider, and so do the eyes of the listeners who are seated all around. The little children stare, their eyes widest of all, their mouths forming tiny "Oh's."

I have no idea what the old woman is saying. The language is completely different, the words nothing like our English language. Some words seem to come from the very back of her throat and she makes these smacking and popping sounds. I do know that whatever she's saying must be pretty intense. Her voice becomes quiet and slows once more. She is making stealthy crawling gestures with her arms, like someone creeping along the floor. Then she stands, spilling poor Poos onto the floor. She raises her arms above her head and stares intently at one of the children — the same little boy who I saw playing the chasing game when we first arrived at the village. He looks really freaked out, especially when she heads toward him with her hands waving violently over her head, her footsteps big, heavy and exaggerated.

A little girl starts to cry, but is cuddled into silence by a girl who could be her older sister. Great-grandmother stops in front of the little boy and stares down at him from above. Although she isn't physically tall, her presence seems huge and powerful. The little boy cowers behind his mother and covers his eyes with his hands. It really bugs me that his mother just sits there, not comforting him much at all. What's with that? I have a sudden urge to tell the old woman to stop being such a bully. Then I notice the small opening between two of his fingers so that he can still watch what's going on. Kind of the way I watch scary movies; I don't want to see but at the same time I have to look.

Suddenly great-grandmother shudders and utters a loud piercing cry that rattles the entire longhouse and sends Poos running for cover. A few people gasp in surprise. Not knowing what she is saying makes me a bit nervous, but at the same time I'm fascinated. I really want to know why she cried out like some kind of monster, but there's no way I'm going to interrupt now to ask anyone. Especially not Yisella, who is watching as if she doesn't dare breathe.

A moment later, everyone is silent and great-grandmother is quiet and still. I'm pretty sure that her story has ended but, just as I allow my muscles to relax a bit, she cackles, scoops up the little boy like he's kindling, and runs out through the door. I can hear him screaming outside, while another child inside the longhouse starts to cry. I get this rush of adrenaline and look to Yisella who still hasn't moved from her spot. I don't know what to do. I want to rush out the door and save the little boy. What sort of a story is this? That old lady is obviously crazy and everyone else must be scared of her because no one's moving. No one is doing anything. They just sit there like statues, as though waiting for something else to happen. Well I may not know what's going on, but I know one thing for sure: I can't just sit here and let something awful happen to that little kid!

The once calm and golden atmosphere inside the longhouse now seems smoky and dark, claustrophobic. I'm about to jump up and run after them, but then they come back through the door. The old woman is laughing and holding the little boy's hand. He is also laughing now, although his eyes are still sort of wide and staring.

Everybody seated in the circle breathes a sigh of relief and laughs loudly along with the old woman. They yell and slap their hands on their laps. Two of the smallest children, no longer crying, are curiously watching all the laughing faces, not quite sure what to make of it all. They aren't the only ones. I can't figure it out either.

No longer transfixed by the storytelling, Yisella touches my arm, kind of like she's trying to apologize, but I know she's fighting to keep from laughing at me.

"Don't worry, Hannah," she says, smiling at my serious expression. "My great-grandmother tells this story over and over again so most of us know it well. For some of the little children, it is the first telling."

"But they're so young!" I stammer. "They were really scared!"

"Yes," she agrees. "They were very scared. It was good to see," she tells me calmly.

"What? Since when is it cool to scare little kids?" I say indignantly, aware that my outburst is turning some heads.

When Yisella only laughs at me again, my face grows hot, and it's not from being so close to the fire! If there's one thing I hate, it's when people are cruel to kids and animals.

"Hannah, you shouldn't be so upset. It's the way it's supposed to be. Little kids have to learn the stories. Especially this story," Yisella says in a more serious tone. "It's for their own good."

For their own good. I hate that expression. I hear parents using it all the time, and nine times out of ten, their reason turns out to be something lame. "But why? Why do they need to be so scared?" I ask, in a voice much louder than I intended it to be.

"Because it is the story of Thumquas! Children need to learn about Thumquas as soon as they're old enough to understand."

"Thumquas?" I ask.

"Yes, half-man, half-beast," Yisella explains. "He lives here in the woods and he's big and hairy. He also has a very strong smell. It's best that little kids know about him as soon as they're able to understand. That way they won't go into the woods alone where he may be able to hurt them. They must learn to stay near the villages."

"Thumquas? He sounds like the Sasquatch!"

Yisella nods. "Yes, Sesquac is another name. Maybe it is the same. There are lots of different names for him, but to us he is Thumquas and he's to be feared."

I don't believe this! Not the Sasquatch stuff again. I have

to fight not to roll my eyes. Yisella gives me a serious look, as if to let me know that she doesn't appreciate my cynical attitude, so I turn my attention back to the group.

They sit quietly once again. Yisella's great-grandmother is among them, now seated on the floor with her eyes half-closed. Yisella whispers that the old woman becomes very tired after she tells the story of Thumquas. It takes a lot out of her.

Several more elders speak at the fire circle. They talk slowly and for a long time, often speaking so quietly that it's really hard for me to hear them, not that I know what they're saying. Yisella sits beside me and translates the important parts. They tell stories about the thunderbird and others about the salmon, like the ones carved onto the spindle whorl. One elder tells a long story about the first human, Syalutsa, who fell from the sky after the Great Flood. He was very smart and taught the ancestors how to make the river weirs to catch fish as well as how to track and hunt for deer. The children all listen, quiet as mice, and when the story is finished, they all shoot pretend arrows at each other and want to go up the river and catch a hundred fish each. I have to admit it's pretty cute.

When it grows dark, and many of the kids are getting sleepy, Yisella gets up to speak. Her people seem surprised, so I guess it isn't often that someone her age speaks during the whole fire circle thing. But she did say it's unusual to have one in the summer, so maybe this one is different. Yisella wants to talk, and does she ever — for what seems like a really long time! Everyone else listens patiently but I'm so tired, I can't stop yawning. I'm not used to just sitting and chilling for hours at a time. Still, I guess when you don't have Google and YouTube and iTunes, you just talk a lot.

I open my eyes as Yisella sits down beside me. I must have dozed off.

"Was my story that boring, Hannah?" Yisella jokes.

"Sorry, but I think I've heard it before," I say with a sheepish grin.

Yisella laughs and then says, matter-of-factly, "It will be fine for you to be here now."

"It will?" I hadn't really been aware that it might not be.

"They'll trust you now because I told them that we were in each other's dreams." She adds, "I told them about the raven, and they know that you're here to help."

"To help? But how can I help? What do you need help with? What am I supposed to do?" I wonder what Yisella knows that I don't.

"I'm not sure yet, but we'll find out. When the time is right we'll know why you're here," Yisella says, motioning toward the door. "The raven has given us magic talk. He wouldn't do that unless there was a good reason for it."

I glance over and see that the raven is there, standing on a piece of driftwood just outside the doorway, dividing his gaze between us and the ocean. It occurs to me that he should have a name. I'm sick of calling him "the raven," so I call him Jack. Probably a dumb name for a magical and all-powerful raven, but it just came to me and, for some reason, seems to suit him. He reminds me a lot of Sadie, the parrot at the marina — the way he holds his head to one side when he looks at you, as if he knows exactly what you're thinking.

"Did you tell everyone about the spindle whorl?" I ask, remembering the electric feeling that flowed through my fingers earlier when I picked it up.

"No."

"Why not?" I can't believe that she didn't tell them how I came to be in their village in the first place! Surely finding Skeepla's spindle whorl in a cave was kind of an important detail to just forget to mention?

"I don't know," Yisella tells me. "I didn't feel it was the right time to mention it. I'm sure we'll know when it is."

"But you can't know that for sure, Yisella. We need to find out what's going on now." I'm feeling a bit frantic, not at all calm like Yisella seems to be. How can she be taking all this in stride? Doesn't she want answers too?

She pokes me in the ribs. "Your mind is always so busy, Hannah. Try not to think so much, then you'll see things more clearly."

"You sound like my Aunt Maddie," I tell her. Aunt Maddie meditates and has a little bronze Buddha figurine on the dashboard of her Volkswagen. She's always going on about mantras and blocked energy and chi and stuff.

Yisella pats my arm. "Come on. The sun has set a while ago. You must be so tired. I'll show you where you can sleep."

Within no time at all, I'm lying on a platform, on a soft cedar mat, with a heavy woven blanket over me. Yisella lies on a mat a few feet away, and it isn't long before I can tell she's fast asleep by the way she's breathing. In a few more minutes, everyone is asleep except me. Thanks to my power nap earlier, I lie awake listening to the wind blowing up the beach and I try to unscramble my brain.

My journal! I almost forgot about my journal! I feel around in the dark until I find my backpack and then reach inside until my hand comes to rest on the familiar smooth cover. I sit up and open it on my lap. Instinctively, I reach over beside me to switch on a light. Duh. Of course there's no light here. And I don't know anything about those ooly-whatever-they're-called lamp fish that Jim Williams talked about. But I do remember my key ring. I fish around in my backpack again, making as little noise as possible, and pull out the orange ceramic starfish attached to my houseboat key, my bike lock key, our marina storage locker key, and — voilà — my handy dandy mini-flashlight. I whisper a quiet thank you to Santa Dad, who put it in my stocking last Christmas.

Thursday (I think, but I can't be sure), June 18, 2010
(although I'm pretty sure that it's the middle of
August where I am, and I'm pretty sure it isn't 2010)

Dear Diary:

Before today, if anyone told me that time travel was real I
would have called them capital "N" nuts. Well, looks like

those days are over. Because here I am, in Cowichan Bay, but it sure isn't 2010. I'm not sure what year it is, but I'm guessing it's eighteen hundred and something or other. It sort of all makes sense now. You know, the dreams and the raven calls and finding the spindle whorl and hearing a girl's voice calling me. It really was real. I'm not a psycho after all! The girl is Yisella and she lives here. Or lived here. Or . . . you see what I mean? How confusing is this? It's crazy.

And Jack is here too. You know, the raven. I call him Jack now. I wish I could explain all this stuff but I don't have a clue what I'm doing or why I'm here. All I know is that Yisella was expecting me. At least that's what she told me. The people here are really cool, and don't seem to be that bothered by me, at least not now. I wonder why everyone seems so chill about all of this except for me? Maybe I missed something when I fell asleep during the fire circle. Oh yeah . . . I'll write about the fire circle tomorrow 'cause right now I feel like a zombie.

I stuff my journal back in my pack and shut off my key light. No wonder they keep the fire going all the time. It's really dark out, and really quiet. There are no voices from nearby boats. No clacketty-clack of fingers on a keyboard. Nothing is moving, everything is still — too still, if you ask me — I'm not used to quiet like this.

17

Hwunitum

֍

I KNOW IT'S EARLY when I wake up in the morning because the light is still faint and watery. I hear gulls screeching on the beach, and voices, men's voices. They're loud, and some of them seem upset. It sounds like there are quite a few people already down on the beach even though the day has only just started.

I sit up and when I glance around in the soft light of the longhouse, I see that Skeepla is already up, working around the fire. She looks even more tired this morning than she did last night. She moves slowly and uses two flat wet paddles to lift large smooth stones out of the fire that burned all night.

She places them into a beautifully carved wooden box filled with water. The box hisses loudly when the rocks hit the water, and steam surrounds her for a few brief seconds. It looks like she fades away and then comes back into focus. She repeats this one more time and I hear the water in the box sputter to a boil. Skeepla adds more rocks until the water bubbles furiously and then she drops a few handfuls of small butter clams into the water.

The sound of the men's voices on the beach grows even louder and she looks up, stopping for a moment to listen. Even Nutsa, who is either kind of bored and don't-carish or giving me dirty looks, comes to life and pays full attention to the voices coming from the bay.

Skeepla looks at me as though she wants to say something, but she doesn't. I wouldn't understand her anyway. I look around for Yisella but she's nowhere to be seen. A few members of her family are still sleeping but several are sitting up and listening too. I recognize the voice of the headman — he's sort of a chief but not really. Yisella told me that every house has a headman who kind of acts like the organizer of the house. I always thought all First Nations people had just one chief, but the way they do it here in Tl'ulpalus seems better. More fair.

I look around the inside of the longhouse. No one says anything to anyone; they're just listening. Whatever these men are talking about out there must be pretty important.

I decide to get up and investigate, because no one seems

to be that keen on checking anything out. I dust off my jeans which are really grubby and damp and totally disgusting now, and try to pat down my ridiculous hair. I know it won't do any good but I go through the motions anyway.

When I poke my head outside, my nose fills with smells of salt and seaweed. There's a heavy mist in the air, and the sky is dull and dark and a strong breeze has kicked up — not unusual weather for Cowichan Bay. I know these mornings well and I'm amazed that even though I'm in a different time, it is definitely the same place. The sounds, the smells, the feel of the bay are all so familiar to me as I step out into the cold morning air. I feel better, as if I'm not that far from Dad and Chuck and home after all.

Yisella is down on the beach, her arms folded in front of her and a heavy cape pulled around her shoulders. Her hair whips at her face as she turns sideways to brace herself against the wind.

I also see a group of men arguing at the shoreline where the river meets the ocean. They stand near several huge canoes pulled onto the beach and away from the churning sea of whitecaps. The men appear to be shouting instructions at each other and, as I watch, they stop what they're doing again and again to look up and down the bay. Yisella sees me approach, and waves for me to join her.

"Yisella?" I yell against the increasing wind and the crash of the waves. "What's going on? What's everyone doing?"

She narrows her eyes and pulls her cape around her more

closely in an effort to keep out the chill. "Not sure yet," she says, straining to listen, "but it sounds like some of the men want to go up the bay to trade with the *hwunitum*. There are more *hwunitum* who live up that way."

"But why do they sound so mad?" I ask, just as Yisella's father, Squwam, smacks the side of a sturdy canoe with his paddle and yells at a younger man. Squwam is usually pretty quiet, at least so far, so it startles me to see him so angry. The young man, who is leaning on the other side of the canoe, shouts back.

Yisella sees this and says, "Some of them don't think it's a good idea to trade for so many *hwunitum* things. It's risky. There's a bad sickness in some of the other villages, and my father thinks we should be satisfied with the things we already have. He thinks that so much change for our families isn't a good thing." Yisella's forehead is wrinkled with concentration, almost as though she doesn't quite know how she feels about it herself. Her eyes take on a faraway look. "No, some things are good. Flour and sugar are good to have for bannock. And Auntie has a white woman's skirt that is much warmer than the Tl'ulpalus skirts in our village. And it is so beautiful: the colour of maple leaves just before they fall off the trees before winter. I've never seen cloth that bright colour before . . ." Her voice trails off.

"What do you guys use to trade for stuff like that?" I ask. I think of home and how people at the marina are always lending or giving stuff back and forth. Things like coffee, bits of rope, cat food or jumper cables for when their cars won't start. It's kind of like everyone shares everything even though half the time you'll lend something and never see it again. But no one really seems to care that much, except for old Mr. and Mrs. Turnquist, who whine and complain about pretty much everything.

"We give them deer meat and furs, like otter and rabbit. They seem to like furs and skins the most."

That's when I remember what Mrs. Elford said in school, about how the Hudson's Bay Company had a fort in Victoria, and that there were camps set up all over the place. Yisella must be talking about them.

"Well, it sounds like a pretty fair trade, I guess."

"Yes. But some things aren't so good for us, I think. Things like the whiskey and other alcohol that the *hwunitum* have."

"Oh, right," I say. "Booze."

"Boos? Is that what you call it? It's a crazy name for a crazy drink. It changes your face and the way you talk when you drink it. I think it can make you see spirits and do foolish things without thinking. I've seen men fight when they drink too much of this . . ."

"Boozzze," I repeat.

Yisella's fists are clenched in front of her now and her cape is blowing open in the wind, but she doesn't seem to notice the cold. She doesn't even feel the rain that is falling now in big fat drops that hit her face with an icy sting.

I think of Walt, the old guy who lives three docks over from Dad and me on his big fish boat. Walt fought in the

Vietnam War and people say he's been drunk ever since it ended. It's really sad to see what booze has done to him. Most of the people in the marina keep an eye out for Walt, but no one was watching the night he passed out at the table with a cigarette in his hand. It dropped onto the floor and rolled under his greasy stove, starting a fire. Walt was okay but his kitchen was totally destroyed. Thing is, he never seems to get around to fixing it. Instead, he mostly just eats up at the Salty Dog Café or at the pub.

Yisella and I don't say anything else. We both turn to watch as half of the men leap into one of the big canoes that they pushed out into the lapping water. They begin to paddle furiously against the wind and over the choppy whitecaps, ignoring the calls of the others who have chosen not to go.

Squwam has stayed behind and remains on the shore long after the other men have gone. He watches until their canoe has disappeared around the point. Now he stares up at the sky, his face under full attack from the driving rain, and raises his hands in front of him.

"Wow," I say. "What's with your dad, Yisella?"

"He's talking to the great Creator," Yisella says quickly. "He's asking for guidance. For help."

"What kind of help?"

"He thinks there are bigger changes coming. My father's like that. He can sense things that other people can't. He wants to know how to deal with the changes. To know who to trust," she explains.

Yisella and I head back to the longhouse. On the way, I

can't stop thinking about her dad, his worries about the changes coming. It's kind of like the feeling I had last night. The calm before the storm.

We are back in the longhouse and everyone seems to have forgotten all about the earlier commotion. And they seem to have forgotten about me as well, which is a relief. One thing that I've noticed about these people: they sure are busy a lot of the time. Don't they ever just chill and do nothing?

Skeepla is in her corner, seated cross-legged on a mat. She's holding a long spindle in both of her small, strong hands. The whorl, my whorl, is rhythmically spinning three-quarters of the way up the rod. It keeps the fleece, which looks a bit matted and dotted with twigs, in place. Yisella tells me that those bits of twig are actually softened little pieces of cedar that her mother will weave in with the goat wool.

I see a single thin strand of the spun wool forming on one side, and Nutsa seated alongside her mother carefully twining the cord into a fast-growing ball at her feet. She looks as bored as anything. Not like Skeepla, who is very focused. Her eyes fix on the whorl, and so do mine; its images blur, so much so, that the carved fish on the surface appear to swim right before my eyes.

There's a bead of sweat on Skeepla's forehead and she looks pretty serious and red in the face. She must be in the dream state — the one that Yisella told me about earlier. It's what happens when the power from the carved images connects with the spinner. These special spirit powers guide the spinner so they are able to perfect their talent. At least that's what Yisella says and I believe her, because the unfinished blanket on Skeepla's loom is really, really cool. My mom would have totally loved it. The pattern around the edge reminds me of a similar pattern I saw on the baskets in Mr. Sullivan's office, only Skeepla's is more detailed.

I switch my gaze from the loom back to Skeepla, and as I stare at the wild spinning blur of images, once again I feel my own pulse quicken.

Without warning Skeepla pitches to one side, and the spindle and whorl drop from her hands onto the ground. The whorl rolls a few feet away, pulling the strand from Nutsa's hands with a sudden jolt. Nutsa looks up from her work as Yisella rushes in to catch her mother's shoulders before she keels over, limp and heavy.

"*Ten!*" Yisella screams, shaking her mother's shoulders. "*Ten!* Mother!"

I see the look in Yisella's eyes, wild, terrified, as she turns to me. "Mother! What's wrong with her?"

Skeepla groans softly, not moving. When I kneel beside her, I can see the beads of sweat running down the side of her forehead. Her eyes search mine as though she is looking for . . . something. She takes my hand weakly in her own before she collapses. Her eyes close once again but not before I see her fear.

Then I notice Nutsa watching me, and I don't like the look in her eyes as she stares as me — the *hwunitum* stranger — with her family.

18

The River

❧

A FEW DAYS PASS and the rain hasn't let up for one second. I wake up to a day that reminds me of late fall — definitely not summertime. Before, on days like this, I would usually just read, or maybe write stuff in my journal. If it was the weekend, I might stay in my pajamas for an entire day. My dad totally gets it but my grandma thinks it's horrifying.

I can't do that here through. Inside the longhouse the mood is as dark as the sky outside. Skeepla is lying on her cedar mat, covered with blankets. Yisella, Nutsa and many of the other women are constantly at her side. Skeepla doesn't open her eyes even though she is not sleeping comfortably.

And I notice that she's started to cough, violently, without waking, every few minutes. Every so often, Nutsa shoots me a look that is anything but friendly, and I feel guilty, although I'm not sure why. Yisella holds her mother's head and tries to get her to drink something from a cedar cup, but Skeepla won't take it. Maybe it hurts to swallow, as it did when I had tonsillitis.

Yisella's great-grandmother says something in a soft voice but she's not really speaking to anyone in particular.

"The sweating will help her to fight the demon in her body," Yisella explains to me. "But she's coughing so badly now."

Her great-grandmother steps in and says something to her. Even I can sense the worried tone in her words and her attention now is on me. And now, everyone else is looking at me as though seeing me for the first time. Their eyes are cold, but no eyes are colder than Nutsa's. What did I do? None of this is my fault. I didn't ask to come here.

"Nutsa wants to go and find Kalacha," Yisella tells me. She has both of her hands wrapped tightly around her mother's.

"Kalacha?"

"She's a powerful medicine woman in the next village," Yisella explains. Her sister is already up and draping a cedar cape around her shoulders. Yisella leans forward, gestures toward me, and says something to Nutsa. Nutsa shakes her head angrily, and shoots me an icy glare. I now feel more than just a little uncomfortable. The two sisters argue until

Nutsa finally rolls her eyes and grabs another cedar cape and throws it at me. I catch it with both hands before it can hit the ground.

"You can go with Nutsa to see Kalacha," Yisella says. "I will stay here with my mother."

"Yisella? I don't think that's a very good idea."

Nutsa is waiting impatiently by the door, looking at me with her usual dagger-like stare. Why does she hate me so much?

"It's okay. Nutsa never wants company," Yisella explains. "But it's always better not to go into the woods alone."

I think of that big dark thing in the trees and I remember how scared Yisella looked in that moment when I first saw her. I have to admit that I'm not exactly excited about going back in there, especially with Nutsa.

"Bears?" I say.

"Bears are fine. But cougars are different."

"Cougars?" I interrupt, thinking about the cougar with the marble eyes in the museum.

"Sometimes they'll follow you. It's best not to be alone in the woods." Yisella thinks she's making me feel better, but I don't feel better at all. Not only is she sending me into the woods with a girl who hates my guts, but now a cougar could stalk me too? Do I get any say in this?

Nutsa sighs from the doorway. She's clearly irritated with me so I obediently put on the cedar cape and the root hat that Yisella hands me. I'm glad to take off my hoodie because it's pretty much soaked right through and it weighs about a hundred pounds. I pull it off over my head and place it over a box by the central fire that never stops burning. I get a few quizzical looks from people when they see the crazy graphics on the front of my blue T-shirt. I'm now so used to what everyone else is wearing that I forget about my own clothing and how weird it must seem to these people.

The cape is heavy but I feel warmer right away. I've never been a fan of capes and ponchos — so '70s — but this one is actually pretty cool. I run my fingers over the tightly woven fabric, and I'm amazed at how smooth and soft it is even though it's made of tree bark.

"Oils in that cedar will help keep you dry," Yisella tells me as I struggle to make the cone-shaped hat fit over my frizzy curls. Of course, like most of the stuff here, it's made of cedar and I'm not going to lie, it's a bit goofy looking, like some kind of grassy wizard's hat.

Nutsa and I head out into the streaming rain. The wind is still pretty intense and the raindrops fall at an angle, stabbing the earth like icy little daggers. On a day like this at home, I'd never be out walking in the woods, and I wouldn't be caught dead in this ridiculous hat. I'd probably just be a lazy slob and watch *Friends* reruns or something. Life's sure different for a kid here in Tl'ulpalus.

Nutsa walks way ahead of me, occasionally glancing back over her shoulder and frowning, as though she's frustrated to discover that I'm still here.

I feel a pang of homesickness as we follow along the deer path, passing by dark green salal and Oregon grape growing alongside. My mom taught me not to step on growing things, but Nutsa doesn't seem to care. She tramples over everything that gets in her way. The trees are huge and close together and some of their trunks are wider than any trees I've ever seen before. A couple of trees could be as wide as our old Jeep. I raise my eyes to follow the length of one, but most of the treetops are lost in the swirling fog that hangs overhead. The light is dim in the forest and my eyes sting as I try to keep up with this bad-tempered girl.

I miss Jack, who stayed behind with Yisella in the long-house. I keep expecting to see him hopping along beside me, or flying from tree to tree just a few feet away. I wonder if ravens get tired; all that hopping around seems like hard work.

Nutsa finally slows down and stops. I get closer and can hear the rushing water of a river just beyond the trees. She leads me through a tangle of giant sword ferns as we begin to pick our way down a steep embankment. I follow her because, well, what else am I supposed to do?

We move, single file, along the narrow edge of the steep riverbank. Nutsa practically runs over the snarl of wood, rocks and mud at her feet. My running shoes are useless as I try unsuccessfully to keep up. I slip again and again on the wet roots. Why won't she wait for me? Why did I have to come with her? I find myself getting more angry by the minute. I'm thinking the idea of Nutsa ending up as cougar dinner might not be such a bad thing.

She stops ahead and peers over the edge. The river below

is moving pretty fast, spilling over large grey rocks into churning pools of deep dark green. Even though it's summer, the river looks really cold. Watching the rushing water makes me feel more than a little dizzy so I turn away from the edge, and see Nutsa looking at me. Her face softens as she extends her hand toward me. At first I don't take it — I don't trust her. But then she smiles at me, and I'm pretty sure her smile is genuine because she looks like an entirely different person. She looks, well, nice. I cast another glance over the side of the embankment to the water ten feet below and my stomach lurches. I've never been a great fan of heights and now that I'm perched here on this sketchy bit of trail, wearing slippery basketball high tops, I'm even less of one. Gratefully, I accept Nutsa's help and take her hand.

She grips my hand in hers like a vice as we pick our way along the edge once again. Every couple of steps she glances over her shoulder, smiling at me as though I'm suddenly her best friend in the world. We only have about five more steps to go before we're back onto wider safer ground when Nutsa stops and turns around to face me. Then she drops my hand.

"What?" I ask, even though I know she can't understand me. "Why are we stopping?" Nutsa just smiles, but not the best-friend kind of a smile. This time, her lips curl as if in a snarl. Her eyes are black and bottomless. I look down and feel a strange pull from the water below me.

"Nutsa?" I practically plead, and I hear the quaver in my voice.

My head spins and then Nutsa is hovering next to me. I

didn't even see her move! I'm confused, and for a moment I think that she is going to hug me. But then I am falling, as if in slow motion, into the river below. My body plunges into the freezing water and the sudden shock of cold rips the air from my lungs. As the water pulls me down, I force my eyes to open to the light above, swirling on the surface of the jade green water. I know that I must get there to breathe. My head is spinning and my lungs are burning as I struggle furiously to swim against the powerful undertow holding me captive underwater.

Up, up, up . . . my ears are roaring and my lungs are about to burst. It's taking too long. I feel so heavy. I fumble underwater, yanking desperately at the strings of my cape until it breaks loose. Free at last, I spiral up, gasping as my face breaks the surface and meets the air.

I am carried on the surface as easily as if I were an old shoe. I struggle to keep my head above water but my foot catches on something. I feel a sharp pain in my knee and then I am sucked under again. I hardly have time to fill my lungs.

"Help!" I manage to scream when I come up for a third time. I reach for a large piece of wood floating out of nowhere, but it crumbles in my hands, rotten and soft. "Please! Help me!"

Just before I am sucked down into the icy darkness once more, I think I see a figure on the shore. I summon all my strength and, ignoring the pain in my knee; I force myself back up to the surface. I gasp twice. Once for air, and then once again when I see the shadowy hulking shape in front of the trees. It moves closer, close enough for me to see its matted dark fur before the water pulls me under. When I resurface, a big alder log explodes into the water beside me and I throw my body against it, my arms wrapping it in a steely grip.

"HANNAH!"

Bursting through the trees, looking terrified, is Yisella. "HOLD ON! DON'T LET GO!"

I do not intend to let go, even though I'm now floating toward much faster and more powerful rapids.

"YISELLA! Get closer. Pull me in!"

Yisella breaks a long sturdy branch off a nearby tree and wades out into the river. She leans out, stretching her body and her arms as far as they will go, extending the branch toward me. When the current bites into her calves and threatens to carry her off as well, she steps back.

"I can't reach, Hannah! Kick your legs! You can do it!"

I think of Dad and Aunt Maddie, and Chuck with a Cheerio stuck on the end of his nose. And then I smell a familiar scent, something good. Lemons! It is all the extra encouragement I need. I kick my legs as hard as I can, willing myself toward the shore. In seconds, I grab the end of Yisella's branch and finally let go of the log.

"Now, Yisella, now! Pull me in!" And moments later, I am standing knee-deep in a slow moving eddy, shivering uncontrollably.

"Hannah. Hannah, are you okay?" Yisella rushes over. She takes off her cape and wraps it around me, and then hugs me tight against her.

"Did you see that thing," I ask, "that animal?" The vision of the dark shape in the trees is still crystal clear in my head. I can see the mass of dark matted fur, the loping gait.

Yisella looks confused. "What animal? You mean the raven?" Jack appears out of nowhere and caws frantically from a low-lying branch on the riverbank.

"No, not Jack!" I shiver and my teeth chatter from the cold, and the fear. "Like before! Like that other time, right after I got here. Didn't you see just now? In the trees? It was coming toward me. I couldn't really see what it was. Some kind of bear! Some kind of . . ."

"Thumquas," Yisella says solemnly.

I don't say anything because there's a part of me that thinks she might be right. Or maybe my brain is partially frozen and I'm seeing things. That's just it, I don't know what I saw but I'm pretty sure that it wasn't a bear.

The ends of my fingers feel numb, so I rub my hands together vigorously trying to warm them up. I stop thinking about the hairy thing on the shore and remember the chunk of alder exploding into the river.

"Thanks for tossing me that hunk of wood, Yisella. I don't know what I would have done if you hadn't done that."

"What piece of wood?" She looks confused. "You mean that log you were floating on? I didn't throw that; I doubt I could even lift it!"

I blink at her. It doesn't make sense. But then I remember Nutsa and my freaky fall into the water. Did she have an attack of guilt and heave the log to me at the last minute? Come to think of it: where is she?

And what is Yisella doing here?

"Yisella, why are you here? I mean, I'm really glad to see you but I thought you were going to stay with your mother."

"I was, but not long after you two left, we had a visitor from Clem Clem. She had heard that my mother was very ill, so she came to help. When I told her that Nutsa had gone to get Kalacha, she told me that Kalacha's village has gone to the mainland already and that Kalacha has gone with them. So I came to bring you back."

Yisella stops talking when we hear a rustle in the trees, but it is only Nutsa. When she sees Yisella, she slaps her hand over her mouth in horror, a wild look in her eyes, and rushes forward. I step back, my foot splashing into the water, but Yisella quickly pulls me back. The river current wouldn't think twice about dragging me out into the rapids again.

Yisella and her sister talk a mile a minute. Their voices swirl around inside my head. I recognize the emotions even though I can't understand the words. Anger. Fear. Concern. That reminds me . . . where's Jack? I thought I saw him earlier, sitting in a tree.

And what about Nutsa? Do I tell Yisella? Do I tell her that I'm pretty sure her sister pushed me into the river? That I think she tried to kill me? Or am I imagining that? Did I just have a dizzy spell and fall? Was Nutsa worried for my life? Is that why she has appeared on the riverbank?

I'm still a little dazed, and my legs buckle. I sit down on the gravel bank, grateful to take the weight off my injured knee. Yisella sees my ripped jeans, and the blood oozing from the gash on my knee. "Wait here," she orders, and darts off into the woods. Wait here? I don't really have a choice but I don't want to be stuck beside a raging river with Nutsa, who is staring at me again.

"You pushed me, didn't you!" I accuse, knowing that she can't answer me. I don't care; I need to say it out loud anyway. She doesn't even try to answer. She doesn't even bother to look confused.

"Why? Why do you hate me so much?" I'm actually yelling and there are tears of frustration in my eyes. "What did I ever do to you?"

Nutsa just stands there, looking smug. I want to slap her.

Suddenly out of nowhere, Jack returns, flapping and hopping around frantically beside us. Before I can say anything more, Yisella bursts through the trees.

"Here, put this on your knee." She opens both her hands to reveal a pulpy wet greenish-grey mess of . . . I don't know what.

"Ew. What is that?" It looks like something Nell's dog, Quincy, could have upchucked.

"Yarrow," she says, slapping the disgusting mess over the top of my knee.

"Ow!" I wince at the sting and squeal in protest as she pulls on my ankle to stretch out my leg.

"Don't worry," she says, "this will stop the bleeding. I just need to wrap it in this." She picks up a strip of cedar bark and wraps it around my knee, making sure the oatmeal-like sludge is covering the wound.

"Doesn't look like yarrow to me," I say, thinking of the lacy flowerlike weed that grows almost everywhere in summer.

"Not anymore," Yisella smiles, "not now that I've chewed all the flowers up."

"What? My knee is covered in your spit?"

She finishes tying the cedar strip on my leg and when she's sure it's good and tight, she looks up at me and says, "Yes. That's right."

"Gross."

"Gross? I don't know this word." She looks so earnest that I laugh out loud and forget, for a moment, about Nutsa. I'll make sure she walks well ahead of us on our way back to Tl'ulpalus. I want to keep my eye on her. I wish I could tell Yisella my suspicions about her sister, but she's got enough to deal with right now, so I keep my mouth shut. I just want to get back to the warmth of the fire and dry out.

We have barely started back when Yisella stops dead in her tracks.

"What?" I say, when she just stands there staring at the ground.

She looks up at me, her eyes huge, and points to the ground. I look down and there, in broad daylight, are two of the biggest footprints I have ever seen in my whole entire life. They look human, only they're at least twice the size of any human foot I've ever seen.

That was no bear I saw on the riverbank.

19

Fever

❧

WE DON'T TELL anyone what happened in the woods. And no one questions why I am wet or walking with a limp. Skeepla is worse, and that is all any of us care about now.

Nothing seems to help her. People are trying all kinds of stuff, and all I can do is watch. I hate feeling like this. I'm not the sort of person who likes to sit around and watch other people work. I like to get in there. This sucks. I can feel the tension in the air. Everyone is silent, casting worried looks over to the sleeping platform where Skeepla moans quietly, her hair damp and lifeless. Yisella's grandmother is kneeling beside her, chanting softly in a deep steady voice as she sweeps the air above Skeepla with a thick cedar bough. No one interrupts her or joins in. She is left alone, sweeping the air for what seems like hours and hours. You can feel the sadness inside the longhouse. What's worse for me is knowing that I've seen all this before. I remember in one of my dreams that I saw Skeepla and this old woman with the cedar bough. I heard the chanting and I saw the beads of sweat on Skeepla's face. But in my dream, Skeepla doesn't get better because, in my dream, she is dying. I really hope it is one dream that doesn't come true.

It isn't long before Yisella's mother breaks out in a rash that spreads over her face and hands, and soon her whole body is covered with strange red bumps. Skeepla drifts in and out of her fever, not able to eat any food at all. I try to help as much as I can but, when the rash turns into big angry blisters, there seems to be little that I, or the people of Tl'ulpalus, can do for her.

The villagers are really scared of this illness. They have heard stories about other people dying up and down the island — how none of their medicines could save them. Men, women and children are powerless against it. I feel totally crappy because I know that this sickness has to be smallpox, the awful disease that wiped out so many of the first peoples on the west coast of Canada. We learned about it in social studies class. There were huge epidemics happening everywhere and there was a major one on Vancouver Island in 1862. Is this the start? Have I really travelled back almost one hundred and fifty years? And am I going to stay here forever? What is the point of all this?

There's nothing I can do right now except be Yisella's friend. But I'm still afraid. I'm afraid because now there are others in Tl'ulpalus who are getting sick. Two of the elders and two of the really young kids have the fever and the same rash, and everybody is freaking out. It's heartbreaking, and terrifying to watch. And what about me? I'm lucky that I don't get sick very much — I never even get colds. But what if I get this?

These days Yisella barely leaves her mother's side. She sits and watches, and on the rare occasion that Skeepla is more aware of her surroundings, Yisella sings and talks to her.

A week after Skeepla's illness first took hold, she wakes and sees Yisella sitting beside her. She takes Yisella's hand and looks her in the eye. Her grip is serious, strong despite the fact that she has become so frail and weak. They speak in hushed tones for a little while.

Skeepla falls back into an exhausted sleep and Yisella walks quickly out of the longhouse. I'm not sure if I should follow her but Yisella's grandmother gives me a look as if I should. It's strange. I've only been here in Tl'ulpalus for a little over two weeks, and yet I can often understand everyone instinctively, in a way that's hard to describe. I can understand and speak only a few Quw'utsun' words but you can say a lot with your eyes, or in the way you move, and in the gestures that you make with your hands. It makes me think that maybe I talk too much most of the time.

Yisella is sitting on the grass just outside the longhouse. She twirls a long piece of beach grass around her forefinger. I stretch my toes in front of me when I sit down beside her. The rain has stopped and today it is hot and the ocean is flat and calm. I can tell it's going to be a perfect summer day.

"My mother is worried. She says that summer will soon be over and I need to get ready for another trip across the water with the rest of the village."

"Why?" I ask. "Where?"

"Our summer camp. Sometimes we make two or three trips. It's the most important time, when we trade for things like the goat's wool, remember? It's harder for the people over there to have enough food during the winter. The Quw'utsun' people are lucky to have so much here to eat."

That explains why I've seen the villagers checking out the canoes on the beach the past couple of days. The boats are huge and heavy looking, much bigger than any canoes that I've ever seen. The large front ends, the bows, are high and each is carved with a ferocious and very intimidating wolf's head. I see men lashing large planks to the canoes with cedar rope. Yisella says they use them to build summerhouses when they reach the other side of the strait. It's hard for me to believe that these canoes, as sturdy as they look, can be paddled all the way across the Strait of Georgia! I've done the trip tons of times and sometimes it's pretty rough, even in a humongous ferryboat. I wonder if the Quw'utsun' people get seasick?

"But someone has to stay here in the village, don't they?" I ask.

Yisella frowns but doesn't answer right away. I'm sure that she's thinking about Skeepla and the others who are sick. "I'm going to stay to finish my mother's blanket," she says in a matter-of-fact tone. She stares at the ground when she says this, which is weird because she usually looks you straight in the eye when she talks to you.

"But," I push, "you said you can't do it. Weave, I mean. You said you don't have the spinning gift."

Yisella blinks slowly. "I don't. But I think I should stay and try anyway. Nutsa can't be trusted to finish it. My mother——" Her voice catches and she stops talking. I recognize the pain in her voice. I know all about that. I just nod like I understand because, well, I do.

Before, when I watched Skeepla working with the spindle whorl, I'd noticed the wooden loom sitting near the baskets of fleece. Two vertical pieces of wood stood straight and tall, supporting two thinner horizontal pieces about six feet long. Over this, was the off-white tightly woven blanket that her mother was working on. It had a deep brown and red geometric design running down both sides.

"I've watched enough to know how to make that pattern," Yisella tells me, looking suddenly composed again. She tells me that the blanket is her mother's most prized piece of work so far, a present to be given at the potlatch. It is an important potlatch, held at the very end of summer.

Our class had learned a little bit about potlatches from Mrs. Elford. I knew that it was a kind of "giving away" party, where the invited guests received tons of stuff. The more stuff the guests received, the more important the party-givers were. Then the guests would have to give their own potlatch down the road and try to give even more stuff to their guests to prove that they were even more important. So the better the gifts you gave away, the more status your village received. Tl'ulpalus was bound to rate high, partly because of Skeepla's amazing skill. Yisella says that this blanket is like no other.

"The problem is that Mother won't want me to stay here," she continues. "She'll want me to work hard with the rest of village."

Poor Yisella. Lately she looks worried all the time, which seems like an awful way for a kid to be. She's worried about her mother's health, worried about her sister's bad attitude, worried about her father and his worry over the villagers' fascination with the *hwunitum*. Wow . . . all I ever seem to worry about is getting my homework done on time and trying not to miss the school bus in the morning.

"What are you going to do?"

"I'm not sure. If I stay, it will make my mother angry. But if I go, it won't feel right. I just don't know what I should do."

I feel bad for her. It's kind of like the time I had to choose between going horseback riding with Gwyneth — something we'd planned for weeks — or helping Nell in the bakery when she broke her arm. I felt sure that Nell would be seriously mad if she learned I'd passed up a party to help her, but I also knew that Gwyneth would be mad if I ditched riding with her. In the end, I helped Nell, and Gwyneth ended up being cool with it. I guess that's why she was my best friend.

"Come on, Yisella, let's go walk on the beach. Sometimes walking helps me figure stuff out. Maybe it'll help you too."

She nods her head but her mind is somewhere else. Yisella peers through the entrance to the longhouse and gazes over at the unfinished blanket on the rustic loom. I look over to where Skeepla is lying. She's so weak now that she is no longer even moaning. It's an awful and frightening sight. Her entire body is covered with the angry blisters, so much so that you can't see a single patch of smooth skin. Her breathing is rapid and shallow, and her arms are limp at her sides. It's one thing to read about smallpox, but another to see it up close. It's like a nightmare.

Yisella's grandmother continues to sweep the air around Skeepla with the cedar bough, but her movements are different than they were over a week ago. Now they're almost peaceful. Our eyes meet and I see something in her look that tells me Skeepla won't be with us much longer. She knows it, I know it; and while I'm pretty sure that Yisella isn't letting herself think about it, I think she knows it too. I look over and I can tell that she's worrying again.

"Come on, Yisella," I say, grabbing her arm and leading

her away from the longhouse. "You've been sitting here long enough." As we pass the doorway, I block the sight of her mother's body with my own.

The morning passes slowly and peacefully. We walk up and down the beach, not talking much, and then we sit on a log, mindlessly drawing pictures in the wet sand. It's the first time that I've seen my friend without something to do and I secretly vow that I will never complain to my dad about the few chores I have. They're nothing compared to what Yisella has to do.

I tell her a bit more about my home, my Cowichan Bay. How there are many boats, but not like the canoes that she knows. I tell her about our boat that we live on, how we sleep on it, how we can cook on it, and how we have a lot of neighbours who live the same way. I tell her about Nell's bakery, and the different breads and things that she makes using the flour and sugar that Yisella has only just discovered for her own cooking. She doesn't really seem that surprised. She just nods her head, as if I'm telling her stuff that she already knows.

And then, for some reason, I just start telling her about my mom. I tell her how much I still miss my mom and that the last thing we talked about on the day that she died was whether or not Chuck could remember what he'd eaten for dinner the day before. I tell her other things too. About how she loved to brush my hair for as long as I would let her, how she used to say that she would "tame" my wild curls, even though she never could.

I laugh as I remember how she would sing to herself when she was super nervous, making up really lame words to songs if she didn't know the lyrics. How she always smelled like fresh lemons because of the lemon fragrance that she used. She put it on every single day for as long as I could remember. I told Yisella how she knitted heavy wool socks in bright colours — bright reds and flaming oranges — even quicker than it would take to go to the store and buy them. Finally, I tell her that I can't bear to be near her things. That they're hidden away in a wooden chest because it hurts too much to look at them.

I haven't talked this much about Mom since she died, and the funny thing is, it doesn't feel sad. It feels good. It feels good to remember her this way, all the fun we had and the goofy things that she used to do. Yisella asks me so many things about her. What did she look like? What was her name? Did she laugh a lot? Did she like the ocean? Could I sing any of the dumb songs that she used to sing?

After a long time, when I've told her all I can, I actually feel lighter, like I can finally take a whole deep breath. A few weeks after Mom's accident, Dad made me talk to the school guidance counsellor. I'd thought it was so dumb, and afterwards I'd felt worse, not better.

Now I take a deep breath and give Yisella a big hug. "Thank you," I say, and laugh when she looks confused.

"What for?"

"I don't really know." I smile, looking out at a pair of cormorants that have come to rest on a log floating in the bay. Jack sits on a rock at the shoreline. He's always nearby when Yisella and I are together, kind of a permanent fixture.

"Thanks for just listening, I guess, and for wanting to know about my mother."

"We're friends," Yisella says, "and our mothers are both special. *Huy chqa* to you too."

"Huych . . . oh forget it. You know I can't pronounce it. I've already tried!"

"*Huy chqa!*" she says again, and smiles her wide genuine smile. I've missed seeing that in the days since her mother got sick.

I repeat the word for "thank you," *huy chqa*, over and over. It's pronounced like "hytch kah." Yisella covers her mouth with her hand and laughs out loud at the way I say it. I get back at her by making her say a tongue twister in English: red leather, yellow leather, red leather, yellow leather, again and again. Then it's my turn to laugh because she's hopeless.

Our laughter is cut short when Nutsa suddenly appears on the bank above the shore, calling for her sister. I'm not sure what she says but all of the colour drains from Yisella's face. She leaps up and then races toward the longhouse, kicking up sand in every direction. Jack leaves his perch on the rock near the water and flaps his wings furiously, trying to catch up. I'm quick to follow, although I'm really scared of what might be waiting for her. After Yisella disappears inside the entrance, women begin to cry and chant. Yisella's father appears a moment later, his arms around both of his daughters. His face is strained and his eyes are filled with tears. I feel myself stiffen and I hold my breath, everything becoming real very fast. My whole body goes hot, then cold. I know that my nightmare has come true. Skeepla is gone.

Yisella's grandmother embraces her and says something in a very quiet voice. With a solemn face, Yisella translates: Skeepla is now among the people who have gone to the dead. It sounds creepy to say something like that, but Yisella says this is what happens when somebody dies. And that we have to be careful of what we do in the next few hours, so we don't lead Skeepla's soul back to us. If she's not ready to go, she could return and try to take someone she loves with her to keep her company on her journey. I look over at Yisella and wonder if she's scared but, as usual, she looks like she can handle anything. For sure, I don't want her to know how scared I am.

There's so much sadness in the longhouse. No one understands this awful sickness that has taken Skeepla and so many others in the neighbouring villages. There's a lot of talk about people dying in places across the water too. I can't take my eyes off Skeepla's still small body lying on her sleeping platform. She looks peaceful, as if, without the pain, she can finally rest. Yisella and Nutsa sit quietly by her side, ready to do whatever is needed. Even Nutsa has lost her usual faraway expression and she looks alert and determined. Yisella's great-grandmother begins to apply thick red and black streaks on Skeepla's cheeks, talking quietly to her great-granddaughters while she works.

"Great-grandmother says that death is part of life," Yisella explains. "When one of us leaves, we make room for another one to be born."

I can't stop the tear that slides down my cheek. I'm not a fan of death. I brush my arm quickly across my face and give her a weak smile. Her words make sense and I really want to believe them. More than anything. I wonder if my mom believed that? Our family was never much into church or anything, and no one ever really talks about what happens after you die. All I know is that it isn't fair that my mother was taken away from me so early, and I feel the sting of her absence all over again. Then Yisella says something to her sister, and together they look over to Skeepla's blanket and nod to each other.

I go outside and sit on the beach, giving Yisella and her family some privacy. I wish I didn't, but I know exactly what she's feeling. I remember everything about the day Mom died. It was sunny and warm, a day like this one. I remember Dad trying to be calm and strong while he struggled to find the right words to tell me about Mom's car accident. I could hear people laughing by the roadside up at the Salty Dog Café and I remember wondering how they could be so carefree and happy? How could they be going out for a fish and chip dinner today? How could they act like it was just another stupid regular day? For a while after that I never felt anything at all. It was like I was some kind of robot.

I look back at Yisella's family as Jack flaps up from the ground and settles comfortably a few feet away from me. We stare at each other for a bit, and he cocks his head to one side.

"Jack?" I say. "What's the deal here? Why do I have to be here for this and feel sad all over again?" For a brief second I wonder if he'll actually say something to me. I mean, why not? Anything seems possible now. But he just ruffles his feathers and gives me one of his quizzical looks.

I sit there thinking about how everyone has been pretty nice to me since I arrived — everyone except Nutsa, that is. I'm okay being alone, except for Jack, 'cause I know that there are some things that I just can't be a part of. Stuff I can't possibly begin to know or understand. Like that gross yarrow stuff. I mean, my knee has already formed a big ugly scab, which is pretty quick, considering how much it was bleeding before.

So, not knowing what else to do, I sit in the sun on the beach with Jack. He picks away at one of his feet with his shiny beak while I try hard not to pick at my scab.

20

Whorl Dance

※

THE NEWS OF Skeepla's death travels and soon people from the neighbouring villages near the Cowichan and Koksilah rivers come to pay their respects. It's obvious that Skeepla was admired, that she'll be missed for a long time to come. Nutsa and Yisella greet the visitors with brave smiles even though I can tell it is a struggle. Then, with help from the elders, they carefully arrange their mother in a gentle crouching position inside a sturdy cedar plank box. Everyone has a job to do; everyone except me, that is.

Like so many other times here, I feel useless. I'm not sure if I should try to help or just stay in the background. After seeing the looks I get from the visiting villagers, as though I smell bad or something, I decide to stay in the background. It could be my imagination, but I'm sure that some of them are bugged by my being here. Do they think that it's my fault that Skeepla died? Because I'm *hwunitum*? Do they think that I brought smallpox here? I avoid them by playing with Poos a lot.

There's no way that I want to pester Yisella about any of this. She and Nutsa are so preoccupied. They don't smile but they aren't crying either. I think they might be feeling like robots just the way I did. So I just hang around by the wall of the longhouse and watch with Poos . . . and Jack. If I wasn't sure before that Jack was different, somehow special, I definitely am now. No other raven would sit with a little cat — unless that cat was dinner!

I want to be capable like Yisella, but I'm not. I miss Dad and Aunt Maddie, and even the way Chuck chewed on my eyebrow. I feel like the worst friend there is for thinking about myself at a time like this, but all I really want to do is disappear and get back home, now. Poos rubs his body along the side of my leg, as if he senses my distress. I'm so grateful for his company the past few days. I have really grown to love the little cat.

Later on, Yisella and her family perform a solemn dance, chanting in low tones, their feet stamping the hard earth of the longhouse floor. The dance is long and everyone is quiet when it ends, even the smallest children. I watch from a corner, wanting desperately to be invisible. I don't have any right to be watching something so ancient and important and private — I feel like a spy. I'm grateful that Jack is with me, watching.

The village men lift the box that now holds Skeepla's body and carry it out of the longhouse. They walk with it carefully down to the beach and along the shoreline, chanting as they go. The rest of the villagers follow in a line, climbing over the rocks, over the logs, and around the point, as the sun disappears behind Swuqus, the Quw'utsun' name for what I know as Mount Prevost. I remember lying in my bed, watching a satellite travel over the mountain not long after I found the spindle whorl, wondering if it was taking pictures of me and Chuck. That seems like years ago, and not just a couple of weeks. As I gaze at the sky, I know for sure that there won't be any satellites passing over my head tonight.

By the time we finally stop near a stand of trees, the first few stars are visible in the sky and the air is noticeably cooler. Skeepla's box is raised on leather straps, up into the branches of the tallest tree. When it rests between two of the sturdier branches, several men shimmy effortlessly up the tree and lash the box to the limbs, so that it will remain there in all kinds of weather. And, just like that, Skeepla is put to rest once and for all. There's more chanting, and when we're back in the village I hear the beginnings of a steady drumbeat coming from the stand of trees. The drumming continues through the night, long after everyone else has gone to bed. I'm not sure who the drummer is, but the beat doesn't stop, even for a moment.

I am numb and sad, and I can't sleep. I am also really homesick, but I try not to think about that because I know that Yisella feels as though she's walking around in a bad dream. At least, that's how I felt knowing I'd never see my mother again. I can't help thinking how different everything was today. Different from my mom's funeral, where everyone sat so still and listened to people tell happy and bittersweet stories about her.

Afterwards, at Grandma's house in Parksville, I had to comfort my Aunt Laura by giving her neck rubs and some Tylenol. I put up with a lot of hugging from a bunch of sobbing relatives who I'd never even met — telling me to be strong and saying how much I looked like Mom. Eventually Dad came to my rescue and we went off for a walk, just the two of us, along the beach. We didn't come back until it was dark and all the cars were gone from the driveway. Grandma was really mad, but Dad didn't care.

When we got back home the next night, Dad asked me if I wanted to watch old home movies with him but I said no. I couldn't. So we ended up watching a Bugs Bunny cartoon marathon until we both fell asleep in the living room. In the days that followed, some of the houseboaters dropped off casseroles and cookies and stuff, but some people avoided us too. Dad said it was because they just didn't know the right things to say. I guess people just don't get it until they lose someone they love.

I grab my backpack from under the platform and pull out my journal, pen and my key-chain flashlight. My pen is one of those hokey ones you get at cheesy souvenir shops; a killer whale "swims" back and forth when you tip the pen up, then down. I've had it forever but I watch the tiny orca float in different directions for a long time before I start to write.

August something-or-other, 2010, or maybe 1862?
Dear Diary:

Yisella's mother died today. She died of smallpox. That awful disease that Mrs. Elford told us about that killed so many Native people in North America in the 1800s. It's so horrible. Like chickenpox only a zillion trillion times worse. People have been getting sick here for a while, and I wished so badly I could go back home so I could get some medicine for Skeepla! I'm sure Dr. Hall would know what to do. But I couldn't do anything. And I know that some people here think that it's my fault that they are getting sick. Okay, it's not like Skeepla and the others caught it from me, but, well — I am white.

The history books say it's a disease that the Europeans brought over here on the boats, and that Native people had no resistance to it. Yisella knows this white man named

Harris who has a store and a hotel around in the bay. She says he's pretty nice. I told her that we should go and find him. Not only would he speak English, but he might have medicine that would work for this awful disease, but Yisella said he left a while back – gone to get some white man's medicine himself. She doesn't know when or if he'll be back and, anyway, Skeepla couldn't wait. In the longhouse back near the trees, two little kids and two older people have gotten worse. Tonight these men took them somewhere else because the sick can't stay here. Soon there won't be anyone to look after them because we're getting ready to go across to the mainland.

Why do people have to die like this, anyway? Mom was just driving to the nursery to buy tomato plants. She just wanted fresh tomatoes for her famous salsa. Even though I didn't really know Skeepla, she seemed kind and gentle, and she loved her daughters so much. And now, like me, Yisella and Nutsa don't have a mother anymore. It totally sucks. Hey, I haven't written about Nutsa lately and her hate-on for me but things are different, she's different. Since that day by the river. But I don't know what to expect now that Skeepla is gone.

I guess I fell asleep because I wake up the next morning with my journal on my chest. I put it away and sit up, not knowing what to expect today. I see that some people are just now getting up, moving around; others are coming and going in and out of the longhouse, carrying baskets, boxes and bundles lashed together with cedar cords. The sombre mood of the previous day is gone, replaced now with busyness. Only Yisella is sitting quietly in the corner by her mother's weaving loom. She's carefully combing fibres out with her fingers and rolling them on her leg. She offers me a weak smile when I sit down beside her.

"Sometimes I prepare wool for Mother," she says. She reaches into a different basket and pulls out what looks like cottony fireweed fibres. She adds the plant bits to the goat wool, mixes them together, and then rolls the mass out onto her leg again.

"Yisella, who's going to finish your mother's blanket?" I'm thinking about the potlatch her village is supposed to have when they get back.

"I don't know. Nutsa isn't ready. Maybe it'll never be finished. There isn't any other person in the village with the same gift as Mother's."

"Do you think I could try?" The words are out before I even have time to think. I reach out and run my fingers over the smooth burnished surface of Skeepla's spindle whorl. It's cool to the touch and I feel an electric jolt in my fingertips as I trace the carved salmon around the hole in the centre. "Will you show me how to use this?"

Yisella gives me an odd questioning look, but nods anyway. "I'm not very good but I'll show you what I know," she says, and gestures for me to hand her the whorl. She then grabs the spindle, a smooth three-foot cedar pole with a notch in it, and pushes it through the hole in the centre of the whorl. The whorl stops about a third of the way down the spindle. It will act like a flywheel, to steady the rotation of the spindle, and spool the yarn on top.

Yisella ties the rolled fleece to the tip of the spindle and when she is satisfied that it is secure, she spins the pole against her thigh. The whorl spins and the salmon swim in a circle, jumping before my eyes. As my head begins to buzz and prickle, I tear my eyes away from the whorl and watch Yisella work. She continues to work the spindle and I'm fascinated by how quickly the yarn spools on top of the whorl.

I watch until she stops and says, "Now I'll try and show you how to weave. The part at the edges is hard and the pattern makes my head hurt. If I don't watch what I'm doing, I'll lose my place. But I'll show you what I know."

She sits in front of the two-bar loom, focusing on the tight off-white weave of the blanket: where it ends and where the thin vertical warp strands begin. Yisella attaches the new yarn and, using a kind of paddle, she weaves it over and under the warp strands: over two, then under two, then over, then under. She reaches the edge, where the deep red and dark brown pattern borders the blanket, and hesitates. Now she works with three different strands, carefully twisting and counting the warp and the weaving threads before and after each pass she makes.

I can see that it takes a lot of concentration. Just one

strand too many or one less would totally change the perfect geometric design. When Yisella reaches the end, she rests the paddle against the side of the loom. She returns to the spindle and whorl to make more yarn for the main portion of the blanket. But just as she begins to turn the spindle, the salmon barely merging together, Yisella breaks her concentration and says, "Okay, Hannah. You try it now."

My fingers are literally itching to try as she moves aside so I can take her spot, and it's all I can do to sit still. When she passes me the spindle and whorl, I get that funny electric feeling in my fingertips again. I grab a handful of fleece from the basket and my hand feels all warm and tingly. That's bizarre. I adjust the whorl the way I saw Yisella do it, and the craziest thing happens! It's like my fingers belong to somebody else.

My right hand turns the spindle, naturally and quickly, spinning the whorl faster and faster. I control the fleece with my other hand, separating it and feeding it along in perfect time with the turning of the spindle. The salmon start to swim again and blur together.

I can't shift my eyes, and even when my fingers feel tired, I don't break the rhythm. My pulse quickens and I can't stop even if I wanted to. Yep. It's the same feeling that came over me when I first saw the spindle whorl. I focus, mesmerized, thinking of nothing else. I am acting like a well-oiled machine. That's what Dad says when he watches the hockey play-offs. "That team plays like a well-oiled machine!" Which is funny because he's not a huge sports fan, so how would he even know?

Just when my fingers are beginning to cramp up, everything slows down, coming to a full stop. I blink for a minute, look over at Yisella, and see her staring at me with her mouth hanging open. And she's not the only one. A group of villagers are standing near the door watching in disbelief. Jack is calmly perched on the edge of the main fire pit, observing everything. He's the only one who doesn't look surprised, not that I even know what a surprised raven might look like.

I look down at the basket on the ground beside me. What was full is now empty. I look at the whorl sitting on the spindle. What was empty is now full, and the new yarn is even and strong.

21

Across the Water

❄

NUTSA BREAKS THE awkward silence first. She says some-thing to Yisella, her arms dancing wildly at her sides, but Yi-sella makes a shhhsh-ing sound. Nutsa ignores her and talks excitedly to a woman behind her, pointing at me furiously. Soon everyone is chattering back and forth, but Yisella remains quiet, her eyes going from the spindle whorl, then to me, and then back again. Finally she says, "Hannah. Did you feel that? Did you feel the power take you?"

"Power? Well, I felt something. Kinda like I wasn't in con-trol of what I was doing. It was super eerie, but really cool at the same time." I look at my hands as though they're not attached to my body anymore. No one is more surprised at what just happened than I am.

"Hannah, you have the same gift as my mother. Spinning is not easy and it usually takes a really long time to learn how to do it. But you don't need any lessons. You have the spinning gift!"

Yisella may be right. How else can you explain what just happened? Why else would I feel so mesmerized every time I look at the spindle whorl? Wasn't I here because of the whorl in the first place?

I'm excited by the whole thing until I notice the villagers murmuring amongst themselves. They stop talking, look at me suspiciously, and then three move forward to whisper something in Yisella's ear. She looks at me and says, "Some of the people here don't understand this. They wonder why a *hwunitum* child would be given this Quw'utsun' gift?"

She looks at me as though I should have the answer but I don't. I'm just as confused as she is about everything that's happened. So again, I don't say anything. I'm hoping that the villagers are used to me enough by now to believe that I'm just a kid with no idea how she got here or why. Standing by the loom, I smooth out the cedar skirt that Yisella gave me to wear after I ripped my jeans and wait for this moment to pass.

More whispering and then Yisella says, "They think you might have fallen from the sky."

"What?" Fallen from the sky?

"You didn't come across the water like the other *hwuni-tum* or walk a long way to get here. You just appeared. Just like Syalutsa and Stutsun, the first humans. Our first ancestors. They fell from the sky a long, long time ago, and then many others came afterwards."

"But I'm *hwunitum*," I protest, "and there have been other white people here before me. What about the men with the big beards and the "moon faces" that you told me about? What about the people up on the flats who give you goods for furs? Or that man — Mr. Harris — with the hotel and the store? I'm pretty sure that there are tons more down the island too. How could I have fallen from the sky?"

"We know other *hwunitum* have sometimes come on the water. But you aren't like the others. You have the spinning gift. You're different somehow."

I'm different. Yeah, I can't begin to count the number of times that I've heard that before. Especially at school. My hair is different. I don't really dress like the other kids. My shoes are wrong. Hah. If Sabrina Webber could see me right now, dressed in my cedar skirt and cloak, I bet she'd have plenty to say. But I also know that Sabrina Webber wouldn't last a second here in the village of Tl'ulpalus on the shores of Cowichan Bay. She would hate the clothes girls wear here, and the raccoon fat in the hair — no matter how shiny it makes your hair — would gross her out.

I know that I didn't just drop out of the sky, but how I did get here remains a mystery. It's all so vague and foggy. I don't have the answers for Yisella but I'm sick of saying I don't know. I think about making something up. Maybe I should say that I'm an alien from the planet Krypton and that my spaceship crash-landed in the middle of the forest. But no, that's just mean. And anyway, no matter what the story, if I were a villager here, I'd be pretty curious about any stranger who showed up right out of the blue. In the end, I ask Yisella to tell everyone that I'm just as surprised by my arrival and at my ability to spin as they are.

I guess they believe her because they go back to getting the canoes ready for the voyage. Nutsa goes back to filling baskets with items for the trip. She keeps shooting me looks, only now she looks more scared than angry. Like maybe she thinks I really did fall from the sky, and I do have special powers, and just maybe she better be nice to me. I'm still not sure what happened out there by the river; I doubt that I'll ever know. But I don't think she's going to bother me anymore. I smile at her. She doesn't exactly smile back, but she doesn't look at me like I'm the enemy either.

The preparation for the last trip across the water goes on and on. All of the villagers seem to move with increased energy, lashing down baskets and storing cedar boxes within the deepest sections of the canoes. Dried salmon, baskets, more planks for making temporary shelters, and all sorts of items for trade go into the canoes. Yisella tells me that they're late, that most of the other island tribes departed much earlier.

The people of Tl'ulpalus stayed behind to watch the bay for a while, to listen and to be aware. For what, I don't know, but I don't ask as many questions as I used to. The summer is almost over; there's time for one last trip before the leaves fall. Time to get ready for the cold wet months ahead. They must be certain that everyone has enough stored for the winter, because they work less then and stay inside their long-houses more. Winter is the time when they listen to stories, learn special dances and celebrate the abundance of food. Today, even Nutsa pulls her weight, helping to look after the smallest children so that the grown-ups can get their work done.

By the time evening falls on the bay, Yisella and the villagers look like they're ready. Everyone is going to make the journey this time; even Yisella's great-grandmother wants to go. The more help the better when they reach the big river on the mainland.

I know that Yisella really doesn't want to leave her mother's unfinished blanket. She's worried that it will not be finished in time for the potlatch. Although she can be stubborn, even Yisella must accept that she needs to be with her village. And while I don't really know what to expect, I feel excited and nervous all at the same time. I'm pretty excited about riding in one of those huge canoes — all the way across the strait, but I sure hope I don't get seasick. And I sure hope that nothing bad happens on the way over? How long will we be away anyway? What if I'm stuck here forever and I never get back home to my houseboat?

Much later, long after we've all gone to bed, I wake up with a start. Something's wrong. Something is missing. I feel around for Poos but he's not there. That's not like him. These days he follows me everywhere, and he sleeps with me at night. He never moves once he goes to sleep. What if he went outside? What if he went outside and met that great big dark shadow in the woods?

"Puss, puss, puss," I hiss, peering into the darkness. "Come on, kitty. Come on."

"Why are you still awake?" Yisella's voice floats over from her sleeping platform.

"I can't sleep." I don't want to say why. She's just lost her mother, so getting all twisted about a missing kitten doesn't seem like a legitimate reason for not being able to sleep.

But Yisella notices things, so right away she says, "Where's Poos?"

"What — how did you know?"

"If you're calling for him, I'm thinking that maybe he's not here?"

"Oh, right. What if he's lost somewhere?" I'm surprised at how intense I sound. "What if he meets that thing outside, in the dark? What if he meets Thumquas!"

"No," Yisella says calmly, "he'll be fine. Now go back to sleep. I'm sure Poos will show up in the morning."

She's right, of course. Cats love wandering around at night. Chuck often went on little midnight adventures, returning in the morning with a half-chewed mouse or some fishy souvenir for us in his mouth. But I can't settle. I miss the warmth of Poos' little body curled up in the space beside my neck, and the sound of his gentle purring in my ear. How can silence be so deafening? What if he's lost forever? A tear slides down my face. Another surprise. It's so quiet that I cover my ears with my hands. What if he's lost in the woods and unable to find his way back to Tl'ulpalus? What if—

"Did you hear that?" Yisella says, suddenly wide awake too.

"Hear what?" I ask.

"I don't know. A booming noise. The third one tonight. There were two others earlier. I almost woke you up but then they stopped." I hear her feet padding across the ground as she comes to sit down on the end of my platform. "Something is different. I can sense it. I'm like my father that way." I can see her dark shape at the end of my bed and even though I can't see her face, I can feel her staring at me.

"Maybe the noises scared Poos away," I say, sitting up and wiping my face with my arm. "I really need to find him, Yisella. He might be lost or trapped somewhere." Like me.

I half expect Yisella to tell me I'm being totally dumb — that it's ridiculous to go out in the middle of the night in search of a lost kitten. But she doesn't. She's dressed and outside in no time, heading down to the beach before I finish getting dressed. I chase after her as quickly as I can, avoiding the bits of driftwood and rocks on my way.

We stand on the sand, side by side, looking out over the flat ocean. The night is calm, the air is still, and the stars twinkle overhead. Jack stands a little farther down the beach, preening his feathers. How does he do that? Just appear out of nowhere whenever Yisella and I go anywhere together.

I try to steer Yisella back toward the longhouse, "I think Poos might have gone into the woods."

"Okay," she says, "but first let's go up the beach and around the point. I'm sure Poos will show up, but I have to find out more about those booming noises." She disappears into the darkness and I can barely make out her shape as I follow the sound of her feet scrambling over the rocks.

22

The Wait

❧

IT'S THE FIRST TIME during this whole crazy adventure that I feel kind of choked at Yisella. It's way past the middle of the night, I'm tired, my feet are wet again and I'm traipsing after her on a rocky beach with no idea where I'm going or why I'm going there. I call for her to wait up, but she doesn't stop. She's moving about a million miles an hour. Several times, I slip on slimy rocks and fall on my knees. I wince from the pain in my injured knee, still sore from my fall in the river. What's her hurry, anyway? I thought she was going to help me look for Poos. And what's this special "sense" that she claims to have? I'm mulling all this over in my head when she appears in front of me and says, "There! Again! The loud boom. Did you hear it?"

I didn't hear anything. I was too busy being mad, but I can't tell her that I think she's delirious from lack of sleep, so I strain my ear in the direction of the ocean and listen. Nothing. Nothing except for the call of a gull or two and the gentle slapping of the waves on the shoreline. It's the same sound that the water makes when it slaps against our houseboat. I'd give anything to be back there now. Back in my warm bed with my lavender and green striped duvet, with Chuck purring like a little wind-up motor beside me. I blink a couple of times, partly from the salty sting in the air, but mostly from the picture I have in my head of Chuck stretched out with his paw on my cheek, ignoring my pleas to move over. I miss him so much, which makes me almost frantic to find Poos.

"Your ears must be full of seaweed," Yisella snaps, clearly annoyed with me.

Great. Now I get to be cold, tired *and* have insults hurled at me. Seaweed ears. Nice.

"Yisella . . . come on. Can't we just go back to the woods and find Poos? There's nothing out there. I don't get why you have to be so intense all the time!"

"Because I listen when something speaks to me!" she yells. "I care about my family and our safety! I don't want to be afraid anymore and I don't want to lose anyone else!"

She looks smaller, kind of deflated, and I instantly feel

ashamed of myself for whining like that. Me of all people. I remember all the ups and downs that I felt in the days that followed my mom's funeral. Yisella's been through so much. I make my mind up, then and there, to be a better friend.

"I'm sorry, Yisella. Of course we'll keep going. You lead the way and I'll just follow." I find the energy somewhere to follow my determined friend up the beach.

Soon we veer off the rocky shore and onto a hardly-there trail skirting the beach. It's even darker in here, damper, and the roots from the trees are slippery and treacherous. I press the illumination button on my iron-woman watch and it lights up, but it still reads 4:11:26 pm. I shake my head. Really, what difference does it make if I know what time it is? I don't even know what day it is. But I do know that it's August, and that the days are already getting shorter. I even heard the crickets the past few evenings, a sound that always comforts me. Until now, that is. Now their sound just makes me anxious, as if I'm running out of time. But time to do what?

I follow Yisella over the dark tangle of roots and across fallen logs. I'm not used to this skirt yet, so it makes me clumsy, and I trip more often than before. Occasionally I hear a rustle in the bushes beside me and then something runs out in front of me and disappears into the salal. It chitters at me from the safety of the undergrowth.

"Raccoon," I whisper, while my heartbeat returns to normal.

Finally we come to a small clearing on a point, far from Tl'ulpalus village, and stop. Yisella better have a pretty major gut feeling about something to take us this far from our beds. I can see the moonlight reflecting off the calm night ocean and Yisella points to a seal bobbing its head just above the water's surface.

"Now what do we do?" I ask, wrapping my cloak around my legs.

"Now we just wait, watch and listen." She stares straight out to the sea.

"For what?" I sound ignorant, but I don't care.

She answers, talking more to herself than to me, as if she's trying to justify her reason for coming all this way. "For anything. For something."

So, that's what we do. We wait. Yisella watches and listens. It's all I can do to keep my eyes open, and I feel myself nod off several times. I'm jolted awake each time her elbow gives me a little shove.

This time I hear it. Faint, and in the distance: a deep boom. Almost like the fireworks that I watch from Victoria's inner harbour every Canada Day, only farther away. Yisella hears it, too, and clutches my arm.

"Yes," I tell her. "Okay. I heard that one!"

"What's making that sound?" Her fingers squeeze my arm so hard that I think she's going to cut off my circulation.

"I'm not sure. It almost sounded like an explosion, or maybe—"

"Maybe a big fireball from a *hwunitum* boat." There's a solemn tone to her voice.

"A cannon? From a white man's boat?"

"Yes, it happened before when a boat came, not to Tl'ul-palus, but to other Quw'utsun' villages. Fireballs flew through the sky from a big boat with many white sails. I heard this story told when all the Quw'utsun' villages gathered. Twice the fireballs came as a warning from the *hwunitum.*"

"What kind of warning?" I ask Yisella. There's nothing about this in my textbook at school.

"It was a warning that they're here. Nothing more, nothing less. It is why we must watch and listen. We need to be ready."

"Ready for what?" Another one of my lame questions.

"That's the problem. I don't know," Yisella answers. "Just ready."

I sit there beside my friend, waiting and watching. Exactly what for, I'm not sure. But I least now I'm listening.

23

Left Behind

✧

IS IT THE WEEKEND? Is it a school day? Am I in my own bed? I wake up the next morning not knowing what day it is or where I am. The first thing I hear is Jack, cawing madly from an arbutus branch directly above my head, squawking louder than usual. I'm about to cover my ears when I hear the ocean and the seagulls calling just above its surface. I wake up to those sounds almost every day of my life. As soon as I shift my body, I get a sharp pain in my hip, and I feel that my leg has gone to sleep. Then it hits me: I'm not at home on my houseboat; I'm not even at Yisella's on my sleeping platform; I'm lying on the hard ground with a sharp rock digging into me. My knee throbs and I remember last night, how I slipped and fell. I'm miles away from Cowichan Bay, or should I say Tl'ulpalus, on a rocky bluff, and I'm still wearing the cedar skirt. I'm cranky and it feels scratchy.

I sit up and rub my eyes. The day is another beautiful summer day with the sun's rays already warming the top of my head. Jack stands a little way away, craning his neck out toward the sea, the wind ruffling his feathers in every direction. He looks as if he just rolled out of bed too.

I squint and try to focus on the ocean when I see something moving way out on the water. Six dark specks, in a group, are swiftly moving past Salt Spring Island, about to disappear from sight. I nudge Yisella who is still sleeping, and when she only groans and rolls onto her back, I nudge her even harder.

"Ouch!" she cries, and stirs again.

Then I blast her with, "YISELLA!"

She's up like a shot, as disoriented as I was, and checking her surroundings for a clue as to where she is. A look of horror comes over her face when she looks at the sky, to the sun.

"Oh no, Hannah . . . we've slept so long! It's close to midday . . ." but she doesn't finish her sentence when she sees the look on my face. She follows my gaze to the dark specks in the distance and she knows, just as I do, that those specks are canoes from her village. Canoes that will wind through the twists and turns of Active Pass before they cross over the wide open Strait of Georgia.

The colour drains from her face and her shoulders slump. For the first time ever, she looks like she's totally had enough and ready to give up. "It's no good," she says. "They've gone."

"No way! They wouldn't leave without us . . . I mean you!" I shout, angry at the entire village. Didn't they notice Yisella was gone? Didn't they try to find her? How could they just leave her without knowing if she's okay?

"They can't wait for just one person. Not when they were already late to go. Not when everything was right for leaving. They have to go when the time and tide are right. I shouldn't have slept! I should not have let this happen!"

"What'll we do?" I'm starting to panic but the last thing Yisella needs is a frantic friend burdening her with hysterics. I try to be calm, except I know that the villagers took most of the food with them and the cooking tools as well. Tl'ulpalus will be like a ghost town when we return.

"It's okay." Yisella stands up and brushes off her skirt with both hands. "There's plenty of food here. We won't starve, it's summer. I mean, there's lots of things to eat here at this time of year. But we have to stay calm."

Stay calm? Who is she kidding?

I'm amazed how quickly Yisella recovers from stuff. Sure, she freaks out like anyone else, but she seems to be able to pull herself together so much faster than I ever could. Doesn't she ever come completely unstitched and just pitch a fit?

"When they get back and discover that I'm unharmed — that I stayed behind because I fell asleep — I'll have shamed them." She twists and untwists the shining abalone shell on the cord around her neck.

"But what about those cannons? What about the boat?" I ask, recalling the strange booms we heard last night.

Yisella doesn't answer right away. I know she's worried about that too. She doesn't stop twisting the abalone shell. "We have to go back to Tl'ulpalus. We should stay in the village until they return. That's all we can do. I don't want to leave my village empty. Not now. They won't be gone for too long."

We head back through the thick undergrowth of the forest, back to, well, nothing. Or should I say no one. My stomach growls, so I keep an eye out for something edible. I spy some blackberries. They're not the big variety that was introduced later on but they are incredibly sweet. I stuff them into my mouth, and instantly I picture myself on my first day here. Yisella's right. There is plenty of food. If we had to, we could probably live on blackberries alone. I am instantly energized.

When we get back to Tl'ulpalus, the houses already look bleak and deserted even though it can't be more than a couple of hours since everyone left. Somehow, the buildings look older and more weathered. Jack flies overhead and lands on one of the welcoming poles facing out to sea.

Yisella and I make our way up the beach and there I spot Poos, hunkered down in the grass beyond the sand. He looks anxious until he sees us, then he runs out and wraps himself around my leg as if he's a furry little piece of Velcro. I pick him up and carry him as he purrs happily in the crook of my arm. I bury my face in his fur and close my eyes.

"Oh, Poos," I murmur, squeezing his little paw tenderly, "I thought I'd lost you for good. I'm so glad you're back!"

We walk through the village checking for any stored food they may have left behind. We're relieved to find enough dried salmon, butter clams and berry cakes to last us for quite a while. Yisella says that we can pick more berries and she knows how to dry them into strips, a kind of blackberry fruit leather.

We're both pretty quiet for the rest of the day. It's like neither of us is quite sure what to say or do. I can tell that Yisella is ashamed to have missed the summer trip. I think she even feels she may have let her imagination — the "booms" far out on the ocean — get the better of her, although I know she wonders if that something is still there? And what if her feelings do mean something? Maybe there is a reason why she's supposed to stay here at the end of the summer? I want to share my thoughts, but my instincts tell me it's better to leave her alone for a while. Even though she believes that her village had to go, I can't help wondering if she's feeling abandoned. I can't imagine my dad not looking for me if I ever went missing.

While Yisella is down on the beach collecting something in a woven basket, I decide to try spinning some more of the goat hair and fireweed cotton into yarn. I want to keep busy;

sitting around, especially when my mind is confused, is not something I like to do. Also, there's nobody here to stare at me now, like I'm some kind of red-haired freak. There's just Poos following me around even more than he did before. Of course, there's also Jack, who is never far away.

I go into the longhouse to check out the baskets of fleece. Some are still full and I wonder if I'll be able to get through a whole basket at the speed of light, the same way I did the last time. I sit down and pick up the long smooth spindle and whorl that rest beside me.

There it is again! The electric jolt in my fingertips and the heat radiating over both of my hands. I can feel the pulse in my temples quicken. Before I have time to think, the whorl is spinning faster and faster — the salmon images again thrown into a perfect synchronized swim, holding my gaze and steadying my hands. Again and again, without thinking, I grab a handful of fleece, separating it with three fingers as I was shown, and guide it gently into the long strand of off-white yarn. I'm no longer conscious of time. The only sensations present are the sound of the spindle turning on the hard ground, the rustle of baskets and the warmth on my back from the sun streaming through the longhouse door. I feel wonderfully calm, like the way Aunt Maddie says she feels when she meditates.

I stay like this for a time, spinning, enjoying the sun, not really thinking about anything, and then, as quickly as I began, I'm finished. The basket is empty and once again the spindle is full of yarn. This time I don't stop there. I find the goat hair and the fireweed cotton, and I work the two together until I have another evenly mixed basket ready for spinning. I even remember to add the white powdery stuff, a clay-like dust that Yisella showed me, into the mix to make it less oily. Then away I go again, turning, spinning, and feeding, stopping only occasionally to shift my weight or stretch my back.

I know I spend most of the afternoon doing this because by the time Yisella comes through the door, the sun is much lower and her shadow much longer on the longhouse floor. Poos is curled up in a basket full of fleece, which reminds me of Chuck curled up in his favourite spot, the laundry basket.

Yisella isn't surprised to see what I've done all afternoon. It's as if she expected it. She inspects the rolled balls of goat hair yarn, pulling on a length to test its strength. "This is really good, Hannah. It's as good as Mother's."

I know that this is very high praise. I'm so happy; finally, I feel useful. I also feel tired in a good way, the kind of tired you get when you've worked hard and you have something to show for your efforts at the end of the day.

Yisella and I have a dinner of roasted roots, from a plant with a name I can't pronounce, some more dried butter clams and some green shoots of something that tastes a lot like onions.

Despite the bad start to the day, I am smiling when I crawl

into bed. Poos curls up beside my head and goes to sleep with his paw on my eyebrow. It's such a little thing, but so familiar that it makes me feel safe. I think about writing in my journal, but I can't move. I might disturb the cat.

24

Visitors in the Bay

⚘

DÉJÀ VU. I've heard about it before. Aunt Maddie talks about stuff like this a lot. About how something happens and you feel as though it's happened before? Or someone is talking to you and you pretty much know what they're going to say next? Well, when I wake up in middle of the night, after Poos lands on my stomach and scares me into launch mode, I see that Yisella is up. Exactly like the night before, only this time she's standing at the door of the longhouse, straining her ear toward the ocean. She doesn't have to say anything because this time I hear it loud and clear. A boom, and then another one just minutes later, even louder. I jump to my feet as a third boom shakes the ground we're standing on.

Yisella and I hold on to each other fiercely. We both grab blankets and on silent feet we fly down to the shoreline. This time there's no waiting or straining to listen. There on the horizon, perfectly illuminated by the full moon overhead, sits a big ship, its white sails flapping from two tall masts. A dull glow spills out of several windows toward the back of the boat, and although it's still quite far out, we can see that it's totally headed our way! Right into Cowichan Bay!

Instinctively, Yisella and I duck behind a large boulder on the beach. Even though it's the middle of the night, the light from the moon is pretty intense, and there's no way we want to be spotted. Who are they? Are they friendly? And why is the ship headed straight for the village of Tl'ulpalus?

Yisella grabs my shoulders, pleading with me. "Hannah, I'm scared! I dreamed about this. It isn't good. I dreamed that lots and lots of *hwunitum* were coming here and it seemed like something bad might happen."

"What should we do?" I'm so sick of my own voice, always asking what we should do. At home, I usually feel so sure of myself, but here I'm out of my depth. I can't just call Dad on my cell phone or run into the Toad in the Hole for a quick bite and a rest stop. Here you have to think on your feet all the time and act even faster. For Yisella and the people here, there's no time to dither around.

She looks me squarely in the eye. "Will you help me, Hannah?"

"Of course I'll help you!" I tell her, thinking it's an odd question. We're friends, after all. Isn't that what friends automatically do?

"We'll watch for a bit, but only until we're sure," she says solemnly.

"Sure of what?" I ask. How can we be sure of anything?

"Until we're sure that they're coming here. To Tl'ulpalus."

"And if they are?"

"Then we have to go. And we'll take mother's blanket with us," Yisella says firmly.

"But it's not finished!"

"It doesn't matter. The *hwunitum* have taken village baskets before. They like the weaving and the patterns on them. I've heard that they took dancing masks from villages too. And for these beautiful things our people only got whiskey, and some sugar and flour. If there are lots of *hwunitum* on that boat then all our things might be taken away."

I get it.

"You're right," I say. "We've got to keep at least your mother's blanket from them." Even though the blanket isn't finished, it's valuable in more ways than one. Just like Mom's things, hidden away in that chest. Even though I still can't open that chest and look at them, there's no way I'd ever want to lose them.

In my mind, I see the museum in Victoria, full of artifacts collected over hundreds of years. I see clothing, stone tools and photographs of people dancing in colourful ceremonies. I've seen blankets there too. Not like Skeepla's, but similar.

Yisella looks at me, her voice pleading, "All I have left of my mother now is her blanket on the loom and her spindle whorl. I have to protect those things. I can't let them be taken away!"

It's the first time that I've seen real tears in her eyes. She doesn't even try to brush them away as they slide down her cheeks.

"Don't worry," I assure her. "No way will we let that happen."

"If we could — HANNAH! LOOK! THEY'RE SO CLOSE!" Yisella isn't exactly yelling, but her voice is still shrill and edged with fear. I swing around and see that the flickering light from the ship has grown brighter. I hear the sound of heavy sails bucking and flapping against the towering masts. The wind is stronger and, there's no question about it, the bow of the boat is definitely pointing straight at us. Another boom breaks the stillness of the night, followed by the heavy smell of smoke. It reaches all the way across the bay to the boulder that hides us. And then we hear voices. Men's voices, yelling instructions to each other. They're close enough that I can hear what they're saying. I can't believe it — they speak English! My heart jumps in my chest. Who are these people?

"You! On the port side!" A deep voice booms.

"Hold your fire! The captain says hold your fire! No more warning shots." Another voice this time.

"Governor Douglas and the captain have given their orders."

WHAT? Governor Douglas? Governor James Douglas? He's on the boat? This ship! I remember lots of stuff from my socials textbook. It's one subject that isn't boring, so I'm positive that this is the HMS *Hecate*! About to sail into Cowichan Bay with a whole bunch of European settlers! People who want to make their new home right here on the southeastern part of Vancouver Island. This means I'm right about the year. It is 1862!

My stomach knots up even more because now I know for sure: I am witnessing a major part of history and it is not a good time. At least, not for Yisella's people. When they return, Yisella's people will have to move their village to an isolated place reserved just for them. At least, that's what the book said. I remember it clearly because our class talked about how it didn't really seem fair. How it seemed more like a mean trick. The *Hecate* is sailing in now because the Native people are away on the mainland, and most of the passengers and crew aboard know it!

"Yisella!" I say urgently and she looks at me, confused and scared. Although she doesn't understand the shouts coming from the ship, she understands the intensity in the voices. I tell her why they're here. I tell her a bit of what I learned in school. And I tell her we need to leave right now! This time I'm calling the shots. I need to protect my friend.

She doesn't question me and we both move fast. In minutes, we're back in the longhouse. Yisella snatches two large root baskets and fills them with all the dried food she can find. Then she's at the loom, carefully removing the warp threads from the bars. The half-finished blanket falls, limp, into her arms. She folds it carefully around her mother's spindle whorl and places them both in the bottom of the largest basket. She piles food on top to hide her treasures.

She places a second blanket in another basket, along with dried plants wrapped in a thin piece of tree bark. I throw my hoodie over Poos as he sleeps curled up in his usual basket. Grabbing the basket and my backpack, I give Yisella a look that says, "Hurry!" With one last quick check, she is satisfied that we have everything we need.

We stay in the woods bordering Tl'ulpalus and wait, as still as mice, hidden behind a thicket of salal. And there it is. The big ship is right in the bay, its sails now flapping listlessly against the masts. The wooden stern creaks heavily, pitching first one way and then the other. There are many people on deck, maybe even a hundred, and they're all talking excitedly. I can hear women's voices too. The flickering light from the boat spills onto the water, illuminating the sea and casting an eerie glow. It looks like a pirate ship, the way it creaks and lists over as the passengers gather on the starboard side to survey their surroundings.

I take in the shape of the ship now, with its tall, straight steam funnel between two imposing masts at either end. A horizontal line of portholes dots the wooden hull, a few of them glowing, and two smaller wooden vessels hang from one side. We see a group of men wrestling with something, and when they shout to more men at the other end of the ship, I know that they've dropped anchor.

The HMS *Hecate*. Here in the bay, directly in front of Yisella's village. I may be witnessing this historical event but all I really care about right now is Yisella. She was totally right. She sensed that they were coming the night before. She said that things were about to change and I doubted her. Why didn't I believe her? Now I feel so bad.

But we can't leave Tl'ulpalus yet. Not without knowing what the people from the boat will do next. Will they stay or will they move upriver to another village? I don't remember any details like that in my social studies text. We bravely inch our way closer to where we have a clearer view, keeping cover under the arbutus and willow shrubs nearby.

It seems like we are waiting forever, and after a while the night turns to dawn and the lights go out on the ship. A small boat ferries a group ashore, women and children among them, and they wander through Yisella's village with their arms linked, chatting and pointing as though they are a group of sightseeing tourists! They stop to pick up items off the ground, and marvel at the carved welcoming figures that face out to sea. Two of the children imitate the carved gesture, holding their arms out straight before them, and then laugh as they chase each other around the poles. A woman wearing a long, white cotton dress trimmed with lace, speaks to a bearded man in a tweed coat, "My, but it's quiet." She reties the mauve ribbon attached to her bonnet, which seems entirely out of place on this wild beach.

"Well, well, it's just as they predicted," the man replies, checking a watch on the end of a gold chain that leads to the pocket of his brown waistcoat. He snaps the watch shut. "They've all gone to the mainland. I'm told that the island villages are empty most of the time during the summer."

"But how odd! They've just left all their things behind."

"Well, Eleanor, have a look around. I don't see why you shouldn't take what you like. It's unlikely that you'll ever find curios like these anywhere else." The man leans over to inspect a partially carved pole that is lying on the ground. It's the pole that the old man, the naked man, was carving when Yisella first brought me here.

"Fascinating," the man says, leaning over and adjusting his eyeglass, "absolutely fascinating."

The woman returns from one of the longhouses with several cedar baskets in her arms, and joins the man waiting for her beside the tallest welcoming figure. He casts a glance up at the carved bear sitting proudly at the top of the pole, its paws curled forward in a crouch-like gesture.

"Incredible in a sense, isn't it, my dear?" he says to the woman, who now brushes the front of her dress with a white-gloved hand.

"I beg your pardon? You mean these wooden monsters?" she sneers. She takes a step backwards, as if she's worried that the bear is going to spring to life and pounce on her. There's a part of me that wishes it would.

"But, they're so primitive, so uncivilized!" The woman puts her hands on her waist and does a complete turn as she takes in her surroundings. "I've heard that they run around without any clothes on. Women and children as well! Dancing to drums and worshipping the strangest things! Can you imagine?"

"Ah, Eleanor," chuckles the man, stroking his full beard. "Look at you. It's the perfect place for you to do God's work when the villagers return. We'll have a place for them to live, farther away of course, and you and the other ladies can work alongside them. You can teach them how to be civilized, and teach them about Christianity. But Eleanor, I do hope you know what you're in for. I've heard some very colourful stories from men who have travelled into Nootka territory farther north on the island. These savages might not be the most cooperative bunch. And the Cowichan? Well, they're notorious warriors!"

"Oh my!" The woman says, flapping her hand in front of her face. They laugh together, call for their children, and then start back for the beach where most of the others and a couple of the sailors from the ship are gathered, waiting by the boat.

Moments later Jack appears, restless, just feet away, his gaze fixed on the spot where we hide.

Yisella looks at me with her dark eyes, which now seem almost as black as Nutsa's. She does not understand the settlers' conversation but I'm able to tell her what happened. I try to explain what the Englishman and his wife were discussing.

"What do they mean when they say 'we'll have a place for

them to live'? This is the place where we live! This is where we've always lived."

"I know, Yisella," I reply. I don't want to tell her everything that I learned from my history text: how things end up for her people, the challenges they will have to face. Then I see how large the crowd of people has become on the beach.

"Yisella," I say quietly to my friend. "I think we need to leave."

25

The Chase

꙳

WITH POOS TUCKED safely inside the spruce basket, Yisella and I make a dash from our hiding spot to a big cedar a few feet away. We watch for a minute and then, when the time is right, we run again, this time to take cover behind a big rock separating the sand from the forest edge. But then Poos blows our cover. He tries to leap from the basket and as I make a grab for him, without thinking, I shout, "come here!" I realize, too late, that they will hear me.

Halfway down the beach, the Englishman stops in his tracks and reaches for his wife's hand. I freeze, partially hidden behind the rock, and then pull Poos back behind the rock in slow motion.

"William!" the woman screeches, lifting her skirt and moving quickly up the beach toward us. "There's a little girl! Behind the rock near the trees. She called out to us. I think she's in trouble!"

Yisella and I spring to our feet and make a beeline for the woods. She jumps up and over anything in her path, dragging me behind — her hand on my sleeve.

"Good Lord!" shouts the man, whose voice sounds so close. "The Indian girl has got her. After them!"

"Oh, no!" I wail to Yisella, "they're going to catch us."

But Yisella knows these woods better than anyone and soon we vanish, slicing through a carpet of swordferns, deep in the forest.

We head inland this time, following an open deer trail that's carpeted with kinnikinnick and patches of thick moss. We weave and twist through the trees and, after several hours, we reach a village next to a big lake. Like Tl'ulpalus, it is also quiet and deserted, the inhabitants having already left for their summer camp on the mainland.

"Those people might come here too," Yisella concludes. "They could be anywhere. Maybe other boats will also come here now. We should move tonight, after they're all asleep. We'll wait until it's dark; it'll be safer that way."

We stop for a bit of a rest and so we can figure out a plan for our next move. I allow myself to relax and hunker down in the small dark longhouse we picked for our hiding place. I wonder how it happens that I am no longer afraid of the dark. Now I can walk quietly and quickly through the dense woods, smelling the deep earthy smells of moss and wet cedar, and listening for the crackles and snaps of branches and twigs beside me. I feel I'm part of the woods. I belong here.

Yisella and I lie down on the deserted platforms in the quiet longhouse, with Poos curled up inside the spruce basket. I can hear crickets chirping outside and soon Yisella is fast asleep, her breathing steady and rhythmic. I wonder how she can do that? How she can turn off her brain and fall asleep, just seconds after being wide awake. It takes me longer to clear my head and not think about my sore feet. It feels so good to be lying down on my stomach. Jack rocks slowly from one leg to the other on the floor near me. Maybe his feet are sore too. I unzip my backpack, pull out my journal and place it in front of me. I click on my mini flashlight and open the book to a page I wrote back in March ...

March 7, 2010
Dear Diary:

What's the point of math? It's so useless. I'm going to be a writer when I grow up anyway, so I don't need to know any of the stupid stuff that was on that test today. I know I totally failed it! I bet Sabrina doesn't fail it. I bet when she gets her test back she'll be all like, "Oh nooo! I only got 94%! I'm SOO stupid!"

I stare at my own words and blink. I sound so lame. I have a hard time believing that I actually cared enough about Sabrina Webber's math test mark to write it down in my be-

loved journal. I sigh and pick up the orca pen, determined
to write something way more profound this time. I close my
eyes in the dark, waiting for just the right words.

I wake up with my face pressed against my journal and my
pen poking me in my ear. I feel super-disoriented and I'm
not sure what world I am in. I blink several times, then shine
my flashlight over at Poos who has ventured out of the basket and is sniffing around the interior of this unfamiliar
longhouse. Jack is just outside the open door, ruffling his
wings and rubbing the length of his beak against a twig on
the ground, making soft little squawks while he does this.

My mind begins to clear and then I remember. I fell asleep,
but I can't decide if it was for five minutes or five hours. All
I know is that I had a dream. But I can remember only fragments of it, bits and pieces that don't really weave together.
The clearest part is when I'm walking the trail near my
home. The actual trail! I have my jeans on, and I'm drinking
a mango slurpee from Brigg's corner store. Max is with me,
and we're laughing and trying to trip each other for fun. I
can see the boats in the bay and hear the traffic on the road.
Real traffic. And I smell the bakery.

"What's that?" Yisella is awake and pointing to my journal. One of her braids is undone, and she's rubbing the
sleep from her eyes.

I snap back to reality. "This? It's my journal. I write things
in it."

"Write things?" Yisella looks confused.

"Yeah, stuff that happens. Like the way you draw pictures on the rocks and in the sand. It's the same thing, only I like to write on these pages to remember everything that happens to me every day. I don't like to miss too many days."

"Why do you want to put it on your pages?" Yisella asks, sitting up now. "Don't you remember the important things inside your head?"

I think about what she says for a minute. "Yeah. I do. But I still like to write it down. I don't know. It just makes me feel safe."

"Safe?"

"Yeah, like it's something I do every day, and no matter what happens, I know this habit will never change. I'll always write in it."

"Oh. Right. It's like my *sumshasat* necklace."

"Your what?"

"*Sumshasat.*" She touches the shimmering piece of abalone shell that hangs on the thin cord around her neck. "It's our word for sun. I made this necklace from the shell that shines like the sun. I wear it all the time. I don't feel safe without it."

I get it. Familiar things are comforting.

"Maybe one day I won't need to wear it so much," Yisella says thoughtfully. "Maybe then I'll give it to someone else."

That'd be a cool thing to do, I think. I wonder if I'll ever stop writing in my journal. It's hard to imagine.

We sit silently for a moment while Poos playfully stalks Jack on the floor by the door. Jack ignores him mostly, but sometimes he lets out a little warning squawk. Jack seems to be a pretty patient bird. He moves away from Poos, stands with his spindly black legs slightly apart, tilts his iridescent blue-black head, and looks from Yisella to me.

The evening passes slowly, but Yisella and I both agree that it's best to wait until it's good and dark before we head away from the village. Eventually, by the light of the moon, with Poos in his basket, Yisella and I venture away from the settlement on the lake and go deeper into the inky, black woods.

The stillness of the night is broken only twice: once, by the swift flight of a great horned owl as it slices through the trees just over our heads; then again when a doe and her fawn are startled by our footsteps as we round the bend. They spring into the air and, with a few bounds through the foliage, they're both gone.

While I'm comfortable now in these deep woods, I'm still really grateful for the light of the moon. I have no idea where we are. Yisella, on the other hand, seems to know exactly where we need to go, stopping now and then to let me catch up.

When the trees open up and we come to a marshy area, we sit on a fallen log, resting our feet and taking in deep breaths of the warm night air. Then we hear a noise — a snap of a branch and the rustling of leaves. We look at each other and then over to Jack who drops from a nearby branch and soars over the marsh toward the sound. Yisella and I stand up slowly, backing away from the log to the trees behind us. Jack's cawing becomes frantic. We can't see him, but we can hear the swoosh of his wings and the commotion he makes in the bushes.

There's definitely something, or someone, in there. And then a dark shape moves at the edge of the tree line across the clearing, immediately followed by two more. The dull glow of a lantern comes and goes as the figures weave in and out of the tall tree trunks. I can feel sweat on my forehead and I don't dare breathe.

Suddenly a pale light floods the clearing, and its glare shines directly on us. Then a second light appears, and then a third. Yisella and I stand rooted to the spot, clutching each other in a death grip, unable to budge.

"YOU THERE!" a voice shouts. "HALT RIGHT THERE!"

There are three of them. Sailors. I can tell by their V-necked jerseys and the hats like squashed muffins on their heads. They have to be off the boat. One man is massive, and I can just make out his mutton chop sideburns and handlebar mustache. All three hold kerosene lamps high over their heads as they jog across the clearing.

"Oh!" Yisella squeaks, as I grab her elbow and spin her around to face the woods.

"Come on!" I hiss, and then we fly as fast as we can into the cover of the trees. I hear footsteps from behind and they're gaining on us. I can hear their voices clearly too.

"Quick! It's the little white girl."

"Who is she?"

"Doesn't matter. The Indian girl's got her!"

"Come on, John. I can hear them just up ahead!"

I'm grateful that I've spent so much time in the woods lately. We might have a chance to outrun them. I can hear the big guy coughing and gasping for air.

Yisella and I run all-out down another deer trail off to the right. We're almost out of sight when it happens. A strange growl. Poos, who has stayed small and still in the basket, now peeks over the edge, his ears flattened against his head.

Then there's a noise so loud and so close that both Yisella and I jump, our hands clutching at each other in the darkness. I can hear the muffled voices of the sailors to our left. They've heard it too.

The cracking of branches continues along the edge of the marsh, loud and constant. Whatever's moving in there is large and heavy — much more so than those sailors. I gulp and feel my heart beating out of control. Not again.

Yisella inches backward, taking me with her, and I place my hand on Poos to hold him still inside the basket. When we move, the noise in the bushes stops for a moment and then starts up again with such an intensity it seems as though the trees are being ripped right out of the ground by their roots.

Neither Yisella nor I can take it another second. We flee, no longer worrying about being silent, or stealthy, or stepping around any plants.

Then a single high-pitched, echoing cry rises from the bushes behind us, piercing the night. I've never heard a sound like it before, and I can't ever remember being this petrified.

"Thumquas!" Yisella screams. "RUN!"

26

Thumquas

We run blindly through the woods, ignoring the brambles and branches that scratch our legs and our faces as we go. The adrenaline flows and all I know is that whatever is behind us is catching up. I can hear the lumbering stride, feel the ground shake and then smell the dank, musky smell in the air. I tell myself, "Run, Hannah! Run!"

We switch back in the other direction, and that's when we realize the sailors are still following us.

We bump into each other, and I'm sent hurtling to the ground, smashing my leg against a rock. I can't yell despite the searing pain in my already sore knee. Yisella holds the basket with the whorl inside as if it is glued to her body. My heart is pounding, my head spinning, and my chest feels like it's about to explode. I get up and we once again run through the woods, forgetting where we've been or where we're going. We're just running for our lives. Jack flies up and down and from side to side, avoiding tree trunks, flying under branches, and he doesn't caw or squawk once. I'm conscious of the heavy sweep of his wings as he brushes past just inches from my face.

"Hannah! I have to stop," Yisella wheezes, clutching at her sides, her shoulders heaving. "I . . . I can't breathe."

The crackling in the trees stops, and at the same time we hear different footsteps. Suddenly the sailors stand right before us. The big man with the mutton chops is not twenty feet away. His dying lamp casts a dull, barely visible glow on the patch of ground between us.

"Young miss! We've found you. You're going to be all right. Come forward!"

"No——" I begin, but Yisella pulls me back sharply and I shut my mouth tight.

"Leave her be, Squaw!" he booms, lunging forward.

I gasp, not only at his words, but at the sound of other footsteps in the undergrowth beside us. Heavy steps switch direction every few feet. Whatever beast this is, it's so close that we can hear it breathing! The strange musky smell is overwhelming. Yisella and I are both shaking. I don't want it to end like this! Not here, in the woods, where strange sailors are threatening to take me away. Not for my friend who is now so special to me. Not for Poos.

I cover half of my face with my sleeve. I squeeze my eyes shut and then open them again because I know it's impossible now. I can't run anymore and I can't hide. And there, a stone's throw away, beside a straight, tall Douglas fir, is a shape. A huge shadow. The dark shape lunges through the trees, and I swear the earth shakes as it passes. Thumquas?

"Holy Mother of God!" hisses the big sailor, reaching for his rifle.

"Is it a bear?" one of the other sailors speaks, his voice cracking with fear as he raises his lantern high in front of him.

The light bounces against the trees. I don't think this shadow belongs to a bear. No bear could ever make a shadow this big. No bear could reach above its head and break off a limb from a tree with such ease. Could it? I'm afraid to even blink, and then, as if the shape can hear me holding my breath, it stops moving. Is it watching me? Thumquas? The Sasquatch? Does it really exist?

The one sailor raises his rifle, carefully taking aim at the shape in the trees, while the other two make a grab for me, their hands squeezing my arm as they yank me toward them.

"NO!" I scream. "YISELLA!"

But before Yisella can react, a terrifying cry bursts out of the trees. A split second later, the sailor's rifle flies out of his hands and he cartwheels onto the ground. Another piercing cry sounds, and the two other sailors are flat on the ground. I run over to where Yisella stands, horrified and sick with fear. Great gasping breaths shake her small frame, and when I reach her, her knees buckle. I summon every last bit of strength I have to drag her back toward the trees, even while my own body shakes like a leaf.

Looking back over my shoulder, I can barely see the sailors running off in the opposite direction, all three kerosene lamps now lying broken on the ground where we stood just moments before.

Then a mournful bellow fills the woods. And the shadow begins to move, following in our path. Oh, please! Not again. No more. I can't take it. Yisella and I run fast, but the shadow cuts in front of us to block our path, sending us careering off in another direction. For a moment we lose it — but then it's there again, a shape in the willows ahead of us. I am sure I can see its eyes. Yellow eyes. And the smell is back again, too.

Suddenly, we are face to face with a wall of brambles covering a flat rock surface. We dive around it, not daring to breathe, only to discover that the flat rock face is about fifteen feet high and we're trapped. Then I see a small dark opening at one end, just wide enough for a small person to squeeze through.

It's my cave! I'm absolutely sure of it. I recognize the opening, even in the fuzzy moonlight. It's like seeing an old friend and my heart nearly bursts with gratitude. We don't even hesitate as we push our way through, wriggling inside. With Yisella inside the cave, I push the three baskets and my pack through after her. Then it's my turn to suck in my stomach and slip through sideways with my arms straight at my sides.

Once inside, we stand clutching each other, feeling the dank heaviness of the air that surrounds us. I squeeze my eyes shut and take a deep breath, not letting go of Yisella for a second.

When I finally open my eyes, I see her peering through a small crack between the rocks in the narrow cave wall. I force myself to look as well. I can see the creature, thanks to the moonlight, standing silently to one side of the cave, and all I can do is hope that it moves on. Hope that I'm not on this strange adventure only to be torn to shreds by a monster I don't even believe in — didn't believe in. That just wouldn't make any sense. I can see the dark shape against a fallen tree trunk and it's not moving. I nudge Yisella. "Look at it. That thing. That bear. What's it doing?"

"Not a bear. Thumquas."

It makes another sound, and I feel the hairs go up on the back of my neck — it's such a creepy sound. But at the same time, sad. I can't quite describe the noise it makes. A whimper? A moan? It's so human that I shiver. I strain my eyes in the darkness, willing the creature to come away from the trees, into the moonlight so I can get a better look. Thumquas? Could it be? The shape backs away slowly and then it's gone.

Yisella and I stand still as mice, just inside the dark crevice, afraid to move a muscle for fear that whatever was just here will return. It doesn't. It's some time before our heartbeats return to normal and we can smell the damp earth and the salt of the sea again instead of the unfamiliar animal smell.

But the sea and the earth aren't the only things I smell. Lemons. I'm comforted now, and when my shoulders relax I loosen my grip on Yisella's arm. My mother. She hasn't left me for good. I smile in the dark.

With the creature gone, I wonder about the sailors from the ship. They could be anywhere. They could be hiding in the woods, just waiting to find me again and take me back with them. I have no idea where we are and even Yisella is disoriented. Wherever we were headed in the first place has been pretty much erased from my mind during the wild night chase. Did she even tell me? I can't remember now.

"Thumquas is gone, Hannah. I am pretty sure we don't need to feel scared anymore," she says softly, and I almost laugh out loud at the matter-of-fact way she says this.

"How do you know this stuff?" I whisper. "Do you speak Thumquas or something?"

Yisella stifles a giggle. "No, but that creature was helping us, Hannah."

Who's she kidding? That creature probably wanted to rip

us to smithereens, along with the three sailors. Doesn't she remember the rifle flying through the air? Has she forgotten the way the sailors were mysteriously knocked to the ground? They couldn't have just fallen, could they?

"Yisella," I say calmly, "did you bump your head or something? That thing was not helping us."

"It's true. We were scared at the time, but he actually protected you from those men. He stopped them from taking you, because, well . . . they would have taken you back to the boat."

Maybe she was right. Whatever it was could have easily killed us all. My mind suddenly flashes back to my fall into the river. That log that landed in the water beside me, out of nowhere. Was . . . was that Thumquas as well? Saving my life?

"And then afterwards," she goes on, "he helped us find this cave. A place to hide from those men. Don't you see? Thumquas didn't hurt us. He helped us."

"You know? You might have something there," I say thoughtfully. "I was too scared to notice that, but it is kind of weird how we ended up in here."

Yisella sighs and even though I can't really see her inside the cave, I can tell that the tension is disappearing from her as well.

"Know what else?" I say. "There was one other thing."
"What."
"Well, remember I told you about the scent that my

mother wore? The scent that smells a lot like the lemon balm plant you showed me?"

"I remember," Yisella says.

"Well . . . it was her. My mother. She was here. And this isn't the first time that she's come to me since I came to Tl'ulpalus. There were other times as well. Once, just before the *Nahnum* circle, I was missing her so much, and then again when I fell in the river. I smelled lemons both those times too."

"Well, she's your mother. She knows you," Yisella says, apparently not surprised by any of this. She acts like paranormal activity is the most normal thing in the word. "It'll be okay, now."

Just like that? Yisella believes all her troubles are over?

"But you can't really mean that?" I say. "You get deserted by your family, your village is now full of strangers, I almost get kidnapped by sailors, and we come face to face with a . . . I mean, Thumquas. And now you feel like everything's okay? Are you crazy, Yisella?"

"Not crazy. I just think that you can change some things, and other things you can't." I hear her digging in the basket feeling for the carefully wrapped spindle whorl. "The most important thing is still here. And those men are gone now."

I finally remember my own basket. Poos! I reach in, grasping for his little furry body, but there's nothing there except another blanket and some pieces of dried berry cake.

"Poos," I say under my breath. He must have fallen out

when we were running from the creature. He must be so scared, but there's nothing I can do. Except hope that he escaped and will find his way back to Tl'ulpalus. I think of him lost in the deep woods and — I can't help it, I feel so rotten inside — I don't even try to stop the sudden river of tears sliding down my face. Almost since I got here, Poos has been my constant companion, like Chuck back home. And now he's lost. Probably scared. Maybe even . . .

I'm glad it's dark and that Yisella can't see me. I lean back against the moist cool slab of rock at my back and let my eyes close. Something shifts near my feet. It's Jack. I reach down and touch him as he stretches his wings. It's the first time I've ever touched him. He doesn't flinch as I run a finger along the top of his head. It feels smooth and cool. I'm completely exhausted from our terrifying night. My arms feel as though they're made of dead wood and its hard to ignore the throbbing in my calves.

Wiping the tears from my face, I say to Yisella in my most normal voice, "That was absolutely — the scariest thing — that has ever happened to me — in my entire life."

"I thought I was going to faint!" she blurts.

"Faint? I thought we were going to die!" I rearrange my back against the rock, "What do we do now? Where are we supposed to go from here?"

"It doesn't matter now and we don't need to worry so much anymore. Tomorrow, I will go to the lake and bathe in the water," Yisella tells me. "I'll face east, and pay respect to the Creator. That's the way to gain *s'yuw wun*, a special spirit power."

I smile to myself. Don't worry so much. It seems like a weird thing to say at a time like this, but because she seems so calm and her voice is so soothing, I believe her.

"Okay. But I wouldn't go outside just yet," I warn. "Those men might be hiding and waiting for us."

"I don't think so. Thumquas scared them too much. They will not come into the deep woods again tonight."

"I sure hope you're right."

"I'm right," she tells me. "But let's stay in here until morning anyway."

We both sink down against the smooth sloping wall of the cave.

"Yisella?"

"Mmmm?"

"I know about this cave."

"What do you mean?"

"This cave is the one I told you about. I found your mother's spindle whorl here. It's how I got to your village." I struggle to find the right words — words that don't make me sound like a crazy person. "I found this cave one day, and the spindle whorl. I came back with my friend, Max, and some other people who wanted to see the place where I found your mother's spindle whorl."

Yisella is quiet, but after a moment, I hear her take a deep breath.

"Hannah?"

"Yes?"

"Back in your world, what happens to things that you find? Things from my world? Like my mother's spindle whorl?"

Until Yisella asks this question, I hadn't thought about this.

"Well, I guess that the man I told you about, the man who studies things from the past, I guess he keeps it."

"Even though he didn't know me or my mother?" Yisella's voice is a little more strained.

"Yeah . . . stuff that the Quw'utsun' make is pretty interesting. He'd put it in the muse—" I think for a moment, carefully choosing the right words. "In the museum. A museum is a place where things from the past are looked after, so they don't get damaged or lost. The spindle whorl would have gone there. To protect it."

"So, it would be safe there?" Yisella asks.

"Yeah," I tell her. "It'd be totally safe."

"Forever?"

"Forever."

Yisella is quiet then, and before long she falls asleep. I curl up beside her, missing Poos and the sound of his purring. Jack has tucked himself away in the corner, his head underneath one wing. Before any more images of that terrifying chase, of Thumquas or the big sailor with the greasy muttonchops, can enter my head, I drift into sleep, exhausted.

27

Warmed by the Sun

❧

I WAKE SUDDENLY, my head resting on my backpack. My clothes are damp and sticking to my back from lying against the flat rock. There's a sliver of sunlight coming through a crack in the cave, and I can hear a nuthatch chirping from somewhere outside. I blink and wait for my eyes to adjust to the dim light.

"Yisella?" I don't see her. I can't imagine that she'd go outside without me, especially after what we went through with . . . with that thing, and those sailors. "Yisella?" Something is different. The light has changed, the smells are different, and the opening to the cave is not in front of me anymore. The light is now coming in through an opening near the floor of the cave. The opening is just big enough to shimmy under if I crawled out on my stomach. I stare at it for a long time, hardly believing . . . but deep down I know.

Just to be sure, I turn myself around and feel my way back to the other end of the cave. I know exactly where the opening should be. I know exactly how I will have to suck in my stomach if I want to squeeze through it. But there is no other opening. Nothing. Nothing except a damp, rocky cave wall that seems about a hundred feet thick.

"Hey, Hannah! Are you in there?" I hear a boy's voice outside, and he's speaking English!

"Han? I know you're there. If the university finds out you went back in there, you're going to be so busted . . . hey . . . Hannah? I forgot my DC hat. I can't live without it, y'know."

My heart lurches in my chest and I pinch my hand as hard as I can. It's Max!

"Max?" I call out, and my voice comes out all high-pitched and freaky.

"Uh . . . duh! Who else would I be?"

I grab my backpack and start to crawl out of the cave on my hands and knees. It's only then that I realize I'm not wearing the cedar skirt or the cape anymore. I'm wearing my jeans and my orange Quicksilver hoodie. Gone is the spruce basket. And gone is Yisella.

Out in the open, I sit on the ground in front of Max, staring at him like some kind of spaced-out zombie.

"Whoa, Hannah. What happened to you in the past half-hour? You're all mussed up!" Max laughs and picks some grass out of my hair.

Half an hour? Is he kidding me? I look at my watch: 4:40:13 pm. It's working again. I can't talk. I don't know what to say or what to feel. How do I make sense of the zillion and one thoughts that are swimming around in my head? I stand up, and dart across the trail to where a mass of blackberry bushes grow. I grab hold of a spiky branch, not even feeling the sharp spines as they bite into my hand. The berries are rock hard and bright green. The way they always look in June.

I look at Max. He's watching me, sort of laughing but looking kind of freaked out too. His hair is stuck down on one side of his head and he's got grass stains on both knees of his jeans. He's written some science notes or something in blue ink on his hand and, of course, one of his shoelaces is untied. Without thinking, I run back over and throw my arms around his neck. I give him the biggest bear hug ever.

"Whoa!" he says, losing his balance. "What's wrong with you?" He steps back looking flushed, like he's a bit embarrassed.

"Max!" I say frantically. "What day is it? And . . . and what month is it?"

He rolls his eyes.

"Shut up, Hannah. You're being super sketchy right now."

"MAX!"

He flinches. "Okay! Okay! Jeez. It's Wednesday. June 17th. Same as it was this morning. What's with you?"

"Uh. I'm okay," I say, knowing that if I even begin to tell him what I've been through, he'll think I really have lost my mind.

Then I remember my camera and my journal in my backpack. I took photos of Yisella and her family! I wrote pages in my journal! If I show Max that stuff, it'll explain everything! I snatch my backpack off the ground and practically turn it inside out trying to get to my things. The camera rolls out first and I snatch it up and turn in on. My fingers suddenly feel boneless and I have a hard time pushing the right buttons to get to the albums. I start scrolling through the thumbnails. There are tons of them. Photos of the afternoon with Mr. Sullivan, Jim and Kelly. There's a few of Max making stupid faces and there's a couple of Chuck sleeping in the sun on the deck at home. But there aren't any pictures of Yisella and her family, or inside the longhouse, or the canoes, or Jack, or . . . anything! I switch off the camera and flip open my journal, madly leafing through the pages. No! This can't be right! I search back and forth across the blank pages but the last thing I wrote was on June 17th in the morning. That's this morning, according to Max. I shove the camera and the diary back into my backpack. I feel sick.

Max takes a step back from me, looking at me as though I'm some sort of alien lunatic.

"Are . . . are you sure you're okay? You look totally out of it. Like, one minute you're all freaked out, and the next minute you're hugging me. What's with that?"

"I just, well, I can hug a friend if I want to, can't I?" I try to look all cool and slightly bored. It's not possible that this was all some crazy dream!

"Man, girls are ridiculous! Whatever . . . can I puhleeze have my DC hat? I hafta get home. It's my turn to help with dinner. For some dumb reason my mom has made up this chart about who cooks dinner on what night. I think she thinks that it'll . . ." His voice trails off into nothing. I try to look as if I'm interested in what he's saying, but I'm not really paying attention at all. I'm listening to the steady "going home" traffic as it passes on Cowichan Bay Road in the distance. I'm listening to the ferry sounding its horn out in the strait, and I'm listening to a raven perched on a branch just above our heads.

"Blah doo — blah doo." He hops from branch to branch, looking down at Max and me. I smile up at him. He's a dead ringer for Jack. The Trickster. Messenger of Magic. The traveller between worlds. And there's something about the way he's looking at me . . .

Max and I walk out to the road together. He blabbers on about this and that. I take in the sights all around me: the bicyclists that ride by, the blooming hanging baskets that swing from the shop awnings, the line of people waiting for ice cream at Udderly Wonderful, and Nell . . . Nell is there! Waving from her open door.

"Hey guys. Good day?" she calls, wiping her hands on her bright floral apron. I am so happy to see her familiar crinkly face that I can't stop smiling.

"Well, I guess you had a great day, judging from your face!" Nell laughs, "Who's your friend?"

"Uh, Max. You know Max," I tell her, but she chuckles and points to my feet. "No, I mean your four-legged friend there?"

I look down to see a little grey cat sitting by my feet, casually licking his paw. There's a little diamond shaped patch of white fur right between his blue eyes. I feel the hairs on the back of my neck go straight up.

My heart skips a beat. I feel light-headed. It's Poos!

"Oh . . . ah," I stammer, reaching down to scoop him up. "He followed me in the woods. I . . . I call him Poos."

"Puss?" says Nell. "Well, not all that original, Han, but he's sure cute. Better go break the news to Chuck."

"He doesn't look very old," Max says. "Weird, I didn't notice him until just now. How come you didn't mention him before?"

"Uh, well, he sort of comes and goes."

"Looks like he likes you."

I don't say anything, but dig into my backpack and hand Max his DC hat.

"Thanks, Hannah, see ya tomorrow. Remember the pics, don't forget to upload 'em," he calls as he heads off up the road.

"Yeah, yeah. Nag, nag, nag." I smile. I look down at Poos and then clutch him to my face, not ever wanting to let him go! He smells warm. He smells like sunshine. I carry him across the road and down along the walkway that leads past the Salty Dog Café to dock number five.

We bump into Quincy on the ramp but he's only mildly interested in Poos, choosing instead to wander over to the boat where two men are unloading the day's catch.

Then I have to stop. I'm looking at our houseboat and it feels like I didn't leave it for one single second. I can't wait to go inside, see my room and my green and purple striped comforter, fill the old whistling kettle and make a good way-too-sweet cup of tea. I want to check out the kitchen cupboards and see if maybe, just maybe, there's a full bag of chocolate chips hiding behind the cans of kidney beans!

I step over the dock onto the deck and gently place Poos on the ground. He sniffs around tentatively and is unprepared for Chuck who appears from behind a deck chair with his tail fluffed up like a giant feather boa. I'm so happy to see Chuck but when I go to grab him, he darts off down the dock. He has better things to do. I have to remind myself that, for Chuck, this is just an ordinary day. For a minute I'm worried that Poos might follow Chuck down the dock, but instead he jumps down the three stairs leading into our front room. I follow behind and, once again, I need to stop and take it all in.

There it is. The same mess I saw this morning: my dad's

laptop and papers scattered around in what he would call "creative chaos." And, of course, he's left his coffee cup, half-full and kind of gross, on the table beside the computer. I think it's the best sight in the world.

I flop down on the couch, listening for the gentle lapping of the water on the side of the boat. Dad won't be home for a couple more hours today because it's Wednesday — the day that he meets with his writing group. I'm kinda glad that I have the chance to just hang out with Poos and get my brain turned around again. There's so much to process; I can't even begin to make sense of it all. Thumquas! And the cave! The magical place that started my adventure, and the place where it all came to an end. Yisella and I, we found it together. It's where Skeepla's spindle whorl would stay untouched for almost one hundred and fifty years until I came to find it again. I remembered the questions Yisella asked me about Mr. Sullivan when we were hiding in the cave. The last thing we talked about was how the spindle whorl would be safe in a museum. Did she leave it there on purpose, when she woke up and I was gone? Mr. Sullivan said the traces of organic hairs that were found on the whorl were most likely goat hair, so maybe it was Skeepla's blanket protecting the wood of the whorl all those years? I want to believe this. I want Yisella to know that even though Skeepla's blanket was never finished, it played a major part in keeping her mother's memory alive.

I think of Yisella's smiling face and of the steadiness of her voice when we last talked. I hope that she's okay. I think about all the stuff that she taught me. About plant medicine, and different foods and the customs of her village. But she also taught me about sucking it up, and being braver and stronger than you think you can be.

I settle back against the big, red throw pillows. Poos jumps up and curls into a ball at my feet. It's hard to keep my eyes open, especially after Chuck wanders in from outside to join me on the couch. I count three couch potatoes before I fall asleep.

I wake up because I'm hungry. I pull myself up off the couch. My stomach growls loudly, and Chuck looks at me through eyes half-open. Poos doesn't even move; he is clearly not ready to wake up. I check my watch. It's almost six o'clock, and I remember again that it's Wednesday which means I have to get my own dinner.

I feel as though I've been sleeping forever, not just for an hour. I feel this way because of the dream I had. Another one about Yisella. I scan the room, anxiously looking for my backpack, and see it leaning against the lamp across the room. I unzip it quickly and take out my journal, padding back to the couch to arrange myself around the sleeping grey and the snoring orange fur balls that are Poos and Chuck.

The cut-out killer whale inside my pen swims slowly back and forth as I twiddle it mindlessly between my thumb and forefinger. Then I write.

Wednesday, June 17, 2010
Dear Diary:

This is the hardest entry to write. I don't know how to start. Dad says that when he has a zillion things to include in a chapter and he isn't sure what to write first, he just goes on auto-pilot. That means he doesn't think about whether or not it's going to make any sense. (He says that comes later.) He just writes it down. He calls it "putting down the bones." So that's what I'm going to do. I'm going to put down the bones. And the first thing I want to write about is the dream I just had. Oh wow. Here I go:

It's daylight and I can see the outside of the cave. My cave. And then I see Yisella turning sideways as she squeezes out of the narrow opening in the rock. She's hearing voices. Someone's calling her name. It's a woman's voice, a Quw'utsun' voice. And it's coming from beyond the trees, by the sea.

Yisella doesn't waste any time. She bursts out of the trees and onto the beach. There's a canoe just off shore, a big one with a proud wolf's head carved at the bow where Nutsa is standing, waving her arms frantically over her head. Behind her sits Yisella's great-grandmother and her mother's mother. The three women see her right away, and they all start calling her name over and over again, as though they're afraid she might actually disappear. Yisella's jumping up and down on the shoreline and Nutsa actually looks happy as she jumps over the side of the canoe and swims to shore. When she gets to Yisella, the two of them hug each other. Two young men at the back of the canoe bring the boat into the shallow water where they help Yisella's grandmother and great-grandmother onto the beach. The men stay in the boat, but the three generations of women have this giant group hug thing going on at the water's edge.

And then I just woke up, and you know . . . I feel like maybe Yisella and her family are going to be okay. I mean, I hate that stupid smallpox disease, and what it did to all those people back then, and I hate that no one knows what it was really like for them, but well . . . this was a good dream. I guess I'm going to be writing some pretty intense stuff in my BC history report.

So that's about it, diary, at least for the time being. I'm going to go and get some dinner now . . . well, not exactly dinner, but something I haven't had in . . . forever. A giant bowl of Cheerios and milk!

But I gotta do something else first . . .

I snap my journal shut, get up from the couch and go to the back room — the junk room, as Dad and I call it. On one side of the room is an old cedar chest. It's covered with bric-a-brac, not to mention a half-completed jigsaw puzzle of a grizzly bear in an alpine meadow. I sweep it clean and open the lid. There it is, a cloth bag with sunflowers and little brown birds painted across the front of it — my mother's knitting bag.

I lift it out and open the wooden slats at the top. There are lots of brightly coloured balls of yarn in the bottom of the bag, shades of yellow, peach and bright red. And there's my dad's old grey work sock that I remember so well, filled with knitting needles of all shapes and sizes. I close the bag, and lug it through the living room and up onto the deck. After Mom died, Dad put all her stuff away, telling me where things were and that, whenever I wanted them, they'd be there waiting for me.

I haven't been able to think about it for a long time. But today, something seems different. Today I feel tough and brave, like Yisella. I pull out a pair of needles from the old sock, feeling the smooth metal, cool to the touch. Then it happens. My palms start to get warm and I feel a familiar twitch in my fingertips, the same electric jolt that I felt back in Tl'ulpalus when I picked up Skeepla's spindle whorl. Only this time I'm not surprised. This time I'm ready.

I reach down, pull out a ball of red yarn, and begin to loop it in and around the fingers of my left hand. I remember the hours I spent watching Mom knit during winter evenings. The way her needles had flown back and forth, and the ball of yarn had jumped on the floor beside her feet every few seconds. I remember how to do this.

The needles clack together rhythmically and the rows of

red stitches grow fast and even. I'm not surprised. Somehow I knew I could do this, that it would be this way. I look up and over the row of boats on the dock, out across the water, until my eyes come to rest on the spit of land that sits in the bay. And there I see him. The big black raven flying low over the beach. He circles in the air a few times and then glides effortlessly in my direction.

When he reaches the houseboat, he swoops down low and flies right toward Poos and me. I can see the sunlight reflecting off his blue-black wings, and his round black eyes look directly into mine. He releases something as he passes over my head and it drops safely into my lap. I look down at the delicate crescent of turquoise and silver attached to a black leather cord. It shimmers like a rainbow as I turn it over and over again in my hands. The smile on my face could not be any bigger.

I watch Jack soar high up into the sky until he's nothing more than a tinyblack speck that finally disappears behind the clouds.

My stomach growls and I remember about the Cheerios. I wonder what Poos will look like with a Cheerio stuck on *his* nose?

Glossary

Coast Salish

Among the First Nations of the North West Coast there are thirteen different language families, making up thirteen nations. The Coast Salish are part of the Salishan language family, forming a cultural continuum from the north end of the Strait of Georgia to the southern end of Puget Sound, covering coastal regions of British Columbia and Washington, including parts of Vancouver Island.

Huy chqa

This is the Hul'qumi'num' word for "thank you."

Hwunitum

This is the Hul'qumi'num' word for "White Man."

Nahnum

The *Nahnum* (or fire circle) is a gathering place where stories and teachings are shared among the Quw'utsun' people.

Poos

This is the Hul'qumi'num' word for "cat."

Quw'utsun'

The Quw'utsun' (Cowichan) people are part of a larger group of aboriginal people — the Coast Salish. They have occupied their territory for thousands of years. Archaeological evidence dates their occupation as long ago as 4,500 years, but their historical memory says that they have been here since time immemorial. While they have become a part of modern society, many of their cultural practices and traditions have been carried on for generations, and are still woven into their culture today.

Sxhwesum

This is the Hul'qumi'num' word for Soapberry, a native plant that to this day is still used to form the frothy "ice cream" treat that Hannah enjoyed.

Syalutsa and Stutsun

According to the Quw'utsun' people, Syalutsa and Stutsun were the first ancestors, who fell from the sky to land in what is now known as the Cowichan Valley.

S'yuw wun

Through ritual bathing, the Quw'utsun' people could gain *s'yuw wun*, or special spirit power.

Ten

This is the Hul'qumi'num' word for "mother."

Thumquas

The Quw'utsun' people knew of a great hairy woodland creature and gave him the name "Thumquas." This quasi-mythical creature is known to most of us as the "Sasquatch" or "Bigfoot."

Tl'ulpalus

The name of the Cowichan settlement that was located in the heart of what is now Cowichan Bay.

Uy' skweyul

This is the word for "hello" in the Hul'qumi'num' dialect, which is part of the Coast Salish nation's language. The Hul'qumi'num dialect was spoken in the Cowichan area.

About the Author

Ever since she can remember, Carol Anne Shaw has loved to write stories and doodle. As a child, she was forever being reprimanded for drawing in her textbooks and creating cartoons of her least favourite teachers. *Hannah & the Spindle Whorl*, her first novel, grew out of her fascination with the history of British Columbia, and especially its First Nations people. She spends a fair bit of time enjoying the natural beauty of Vancouver Island where she makes her home along with her husband, two sons and two dogs. When she isn't writing, she can be found painting at her easel, walking in the woods, and finding excuses not to wear shoes. You may visit Carol Anne at her website at http://carolanneshaw12.blogspot.com.